CONTRACT TO MARRY

BY

NICOLA MARSH

MILLS & BOON®

First published in Great Britain 2005
Large Print edition 2005
Harlequin Mills & Boon Limited,
Eton House, 18-24 Paradise Road,
Richmond, Surrey TW9 1SR

© Nicola Marsh 2005

ISBN 0 263 18593 1

Set in Times Roman 18 on 21 pt.
16-1005-36719

Printed and bound in Great Britain
by Antony Rowe Ltd, Chippenham, Wiltshire

CHAPTER ONE

FLEUR ADAMS rushed into the café, trying to juggle a portfolio, laptop, umbrella and handbag while shaking raindrops from her curly hair and cursing the fickle Melbourne weather, a lousy public-transport system and men, in that order.

'Hey, pretty lady. The usual?' Billy winked at her from behind the counter and gave her an appreciative once-over, typical of his meet-and-greet routine with the female customers.

She smiled in gratitude as the aroma of steaming coffee and freshly baked muffins infused her senses. 'You're a lifesaver. Oh, and make mine a double today. I need it.'

'Too much caffeine will get you all hyped up. So if you need to burn off any extra energy…'

'I'll join a gym!'

Billy's innuendoes had initially rankled when she'd first found the coffee shop though she'd soon realised he was harmless. Besides, he made the best lattes and choc-chip muffins in Melbourne, two major reasons to tolerate his light-hearted flirtation.

'Oh, well, can't blame a guy for trying.' He shrugged and turned to the espresso machine. 'By the way, Liv's arrived.'

'Thanks.' She scanned the growing lunch crowd and spotted her friend at a corner table, nose buried in the latest romance novel as usual.

Taking care not to decapitate anyone on the way to their table, Fleur slid into a vacant seat and stacked her load against a nearby wall. 'Let me guess. The tall, dark and handsome hero is about to rip off the heroine's bodice and thrust his—'

'No! Romance novels aren't bodice-rippers. They're contemporary fiction. How many times have I told you that?' Liv stared at Fleur over her rimless spectacles, a faint blush staining her cheeks.

Fleur grinned. 'All those books seem the same to me. Lots of hot action, with the main protagonist being men with broad, naked chests and big—'

'OK, you've made your point.' Liv snapped the book shut and held up her hand to silence her. 'Enough of your literary critiquing. How did the presentation go?'

Fleur's grin faded as the memory of yet another failure flooded back. 'Don't ask,' she muttered, as a waitress placed a giant glass and a muffin in front of her.

'That good, huh?'

'Worse.' Fleur sipped at the latte and savoured the caffeine rush, wishing she'd never quit her reliable, reasonably paid job to chase a dream. A dream that would shortly turn into a nightmare if she didn't acquire some new business—and soon.

'No takers for an accountant-cum-life coach destined to revamp businesses and take them into the twenty-first century, huh?'

Fleur shook her head. 'Not one. Seems like the terms ''emotional intelligence'' and ''compliant oriented teaming'' are just too modern for the average CEO. Though one of the senior execs I met this morning did give me a card and encouraged me to call, though I doubt he was interested in anything to do with emotions or intelligence, the way he kept looking at my legs.'

'Yeuk! Sexist pig.'

'He wasn't all that awful, actually...'

Liv's eyes widened. 'Now I know you're in a bad way, letting a lech like that get away with it.'

Fleur sighed. 'I'm just tired of doing the promotional bit and having nothing to show for it.' She bit into her muffin, wondering if she'd literally bitten off more than she could chew with her latest proposal.

She'd approached countless companies, many through contacts she'd gained as an accountant, to pitch her idea to them. After completing a part-time degree in psychology, which she'd initially undertaken to break out of the conservative-accountant-stereotype mould, she'd come up with the brilliant concept to change the outlook of most companies, with the hope that improved job satisfaction would lead to increased profit margins. Some of her initial contacts had received the idea warmly; that was, until they actually had to commit money to the project and hire her.

Liv leaned forward. 'Show me the promotional material you've been using. Maybe I can help.'

'The way things are running at the moment, I need all the help I can get.' Fleur unzipped her portfolio and grabbed a wad of paperwork. However, as she straightened, her head bumped an elbow and the person it belonged to stumbled against her, sending papers flying in all directions.

'Dammit!' a deep voice muttered somewhere in the vicinity of her ear as she bent to pick up the scattered material. 'Here, let me do that.'

Fleur rubbed her head and straightened up, wishing the stranger had bumped her harder. That way, she could have lost consciousness and woken up hours later, when this all-round dreadful day would be over.

'Leave it!' she snapped, looking up at the clumsy oaf who had managed to worsen her mood, if that was possible.

'Mmm…interesting.' Surprisingly, the oaf wasn't staring at her as she'd half expected. After all, she knew that many men found her attractive, though for the life of her she still hadn't figured out why. Shoulder-length brown curly hair, brown eyes, passable figure, average height—all in all, it didn't seem like much of a package to her but she worked it to her advantage most of the time.

Instead he stared at her brochures, flicking through each and every one with barely concealed amusement on his face.

'If you've finished?' She held out her hand, knowing she sounded petulant but not particularly caring. That was all she needed, some guy to patronise her about an idea that meant everything to her.

He looked up suddenly and fixed her with a probing stare. 'Are you the Fleur Adams mentioned in these brochures?'

And suddenly, just like that, Fleur experienced that strange, fluttery feeling that Liv's romance novels raved about, that once-in-a-lifetime gut-churning, toe-curling reaction that signalled *the one*. She gazed at the stranger, wondering at her bizarre reaction, for she wouldn't call him drop-dead gorgeous or anything remotely as flattering. He had dark hair, blue eyes and a strong, clean-shaven jaw, with lips that were compressed in a thin, seemingly impatient line.

As she'd originally thought, nothing out of the ordinary, except for a strange aura that spelled 'power' and captured her attention in a way no man had in a long, *long* time.

'Well?' He quirked an eyebrow as if challenging an imbecile to answer.

Resisting the urge to shake her head and dispel the fog that seemed to have penetrated her brain, she nodded. 'I'm Fleur Adams. And you are?'

'Someone who is interested in what you have to offer.'

His glance flicked to the brochures briefly before returning to study her face. 'Are you sure you're experienced enough to be offering this kind of service?'

Oh, when it comes to you, handsome, I've got plenty to offer.

For a horrifying moment, Fleur thought she'd spoken aloud as his blue eyes blazed with something more than a passing interest in her business. However, it flickered and died before she could analyse it further and she quickly refocused her concentration before she blew this chance encounter completely.

Squaring her shoulders, she looked him straight in the eye. 'I'm fully qualified, as the information you've just perused suggests. If you're interested, I'd be more than happy to present my ideas to you on a more formal basis, Mr...?'

'Darcy Howard.' He thrust out his hand. 'Pleased to meet you.'

Fleur had perfected a handshake for doing business, though she still felt a tad awkward when most men seemed to want to squeeze every last drop of strength out of her in order to prove some antiquated point that males were the dominant sex, in and out of the boardroom.

However, the minute she placed her hand in Darcy's, her nerve endings did some weird short-circuiting thing that sent electrical impulses shooting up her arm. And to make matters worse, he seemed to sense it too, by the slight widening of his baby-blues.

Resisting the urge to pull back as quickly as possible, she managed a shaky smile and slid her hand out of his grasp. 'If you give me your contact details, Mr Howard, I'll call you to arrange a mutually convenient time to discuss your company's needs.'

'Call me Darcy.' He smiled and for one, insane moment Fleur felt like jumping into the air and doing a Charlie Chaplin-like sidekick.

'Here. You can reach me on any of those numbers.' He handed her a business card and she resisted her first impulse to scan it and memorise every single detail about the man.

Instead, she casually placed it into her handbag as if she had enough business lined up for months. 'Thanks, I'll be in touch.'

He nodded before heading towards the door, leaving her gaping after the tall figure clad in a black trench coat.

'Way to go, girl.' Liv's applause penetrated Fleur's brain and she quickly sat down, trying to act as if nothing out of the ordinary had occurred, when, in fact, the encounter with Darcy Howard had shaken her more than she cared to admit.

'About time I had a change in luck. Let's hope he's interested in what I have to offer.'

Liv picked up her novel and fanned her face. 'Phew! Baby, is he interested!'

'What are you talking about?' Fleur feigned ignorance and hoped she didn't blush.

'In case you hadn't noticed, that guy is gorgeous. And he seemed *very* interested in you.'

Fleur's heart gave a little flip-flop of hope—maybe she hadn't imagined the gleam in his eye? However, she inwardly groaned and resisted the urge to slap herself—what was she thinking? She should be concentrating on presenting a professional image to the man she'd just met, not entertaining ludicrous hopes about mixing business with pleasure.

She shrugged. 'Gorgeous? You've been reading too many of those books again. He seemed ancient to me.'

Liv grinned, a self-satisfied smirk that told Fleur her friend knew exactly how she'd reacted to the man. 'I thought you were into older men.'

Fleur took a long sip from her glass and tried to hide her answering smile. 'Yeah, but I'm not into collecting antiques!'

'Wow, he must've really grabbed your attention. So, when are you going to call him?'

Suddenly the implications of her predicament came flooding back and Fleur knew that, as much as her reaction to Darcy Howard disturbed her, she needed his business. Like yesterday.

'I'll do it first thing tomorrow.'

Liv nodded in approval. 'Sounds like a plan. Though I wouldn't leave it too long. Opportunities like Darcy Howard don't come along too often.' She rolled her eyes. 'Trust me, I should know.'

And just like that, an image of intense blue eyes boring into her flashed across Fleur's mind, leaving her with a sudden hankering to grab hold of this *opportunity* and hang on for dear life.

Darcy stormed into the office and slammed the door shut behind him. Just his luck that the one day he'd managed to grab a bite to eat away from his desk in over a month, he returned to a mountain of problems.

So what's new?

Since when had his life been anything but a never-ending list of problems— starting with his parents' death when he'd been nineteen, assuming responsibility for raising his eleven-year-old brother, taking on a pile of debts run up by a father hell-bent on making his hare-brained schemes work and, lately, trying to raise his floundering business out of a financial quagmire?

Just another day at the office, he thought, before sinking into his leather chair and scrutinising the latest batch of reports on his desk.

Despite the business acumen of his staff, the profit margins he'd predicted for the company had continued to fall at an alarming rate, leaving him in a quandary. He'd tried team-building exercises, personal pep talks and a bonus incentive scheme but nothing had worked and the strange lethargy that plagued most of his employees was starting to have disastrous consequences on the company's bottom line.

Rubbing his forehead, he leaned back in his chair and closed his eyes. The image of Fleur Adams popped into his head and he wondered if he was doing the right thing in considering hiring her to save his company. He'd been impressed—hell, he'd been downright flabbergasted—at the services she'd advertised in her brochures, as if she'd read his mind and known exactly what he needed to make this work.

OK, the brochures hadn't been the only things that had impressed him. Once he'd taken the time to look at the woman whose head collided with his elbow, he'd been pleasantly surprised. A pair of worldly brown eyes had stared at him, almost startling in their clarity for one so young. He'd guessed her age to be early twenties, which was why he'd questioned her ability to deliver everything her brochures said. How could anyone so young be that experienced?

You were.

He grimaced, hoping that the lovely young woman he'd been lucky enough to bump into today hadn't learned life's lessons the hard way, as he had. His view of the world was far too jaded for a man of thirty-eight and there wasn't one damn thing he could do about it. Growing up too quickly did that to a person.

Shaking his head, he resumed reading the reports on his desk and hoped that Fleur would call. If not, he'd have to come up with some other brilliant idea to make his company a viable proposition again. And hope to bump into another lady who piqued his interest as much as she had.

Fleur's heels clicked against the polished parquetry floor as she strode towards the front desk of Innovative Imports, keeping pace with her pounding heart. She'd done at least thirty of these presentations by now and should be feeling more confident. However, she knew that her nervousness had more to do with *whom* she was pitching to today rather than her own material.

Strangely, the receptionist barely looked up as Fleur approached the desk. 'Excuse me, I'm Fleur Adams and I'm here to see Darcy Howard.'

The girl glanced up, appearing harassed yet bored at the same time, if that was possible. 'Take a seat and I'll let him know you've arrived.'

Fleur smiled her thanks and received a polite nod in return before the receptionist turned away and punched numbers into a console. So much for first impressions. If this girl was any indication of the calibre of staff that the company employed, she'd have her work cut out for her. If Darcy Howard hired her, that was.

She'd barely sat down before the man in question opened a nearby door and beckoned to her. 'Come in, Ms Adams. I've been expecting you.'

Fleur stood up, grabbed her portfolio and followed him into his office, feeling like a naughty schoolgirl being summoned to the principal's office. If she thought Darcy Howard had looked intimidating the first time they'd met, it was nothing to the vibes he exuded now. Little wonder the receptionist didn't have any spark in her; the poor thing was probably too scared to show any signs of life.

'Please, have a seat.' He waved towards an overstuffed leather chair that didn't look comfortable. 'Can I get you anything? Tea? Coffee?'

'No, thanks. And please, call me Fleur.' She perched on the edge of the chair; as predicted, it threatened to eject a person from its shiny, overfilled surface rather than encourage sitting back and relaxing. Heck, she'd barely been here five minutes and already knew that this man needed her services to revamp every aspect of his business, from furniture to personnel.

He sat behind a monstrous mahogany desk and rested steepled fingers on his chest, reminding her once again of her old high-school principal. Next she'd be hearing, 'Miss Adams, have you been smoking behind the shed?' Or better still, 'Miss Adams, your dress is far too short. Let that hem down at once!'

'Is something funny?'

Trying to control the twitching of her lips, which threatened to break into a full-blown grin at any second, she schooled her face into a mask of professionalism. 'Not at all. Now, where would you like me to start?'

He smiled, a small movement involving an upturning of his lips rather than a genuine happy gesture. 'I'd like to hear what you can do for my company.'

'That depends on you.'

'Oh?'

How he managed to instil so much disapproval into one tiny syllable, she'd never know. However, far from being daunted, she launched into her spiel and hoped he'd buy it.

'Mr Howard, I need to know your company's strengths, weaknesses, opportunities and threats before I can give you an in-depth analysis of what I can offer you. Let's begin with the stakeholders and key result areas—'

'Let's not,' he interrupted, sitting forward and fixing her with a probing stare.

'Pardon?'

He stood up and started pacing the office, drawing her attention to the designer suit encasing his toned body. For a businessman, he obviously found time to work out. Pity he couldn't improve his personality to go with the body.

'I don't need some generic spiel about what you can offer the company. I've already read all that in your brochure and it's exactly what I'm after.' He stopped for a moment and sat on the corner of the desk, looking down at her. 'Tell me about *you.*'

Surprised at his change of subject, Fleur tried to focus her attention on giving him a brief yet professional outline of her qualifications. However, the harder she tried to focus, the more her attention shifted to the man sitting in front of her with his crotch at eye level.

Wrenching her gaze away, she looked up at him, only to find him looking at her with those all-seeing, all-knowing blue eyes. And if she didn't know any better, she could've sworn she glimpsed amusement in their depths.

Clearing her throat, she gave him the abbreviated version of what she assumed he wanted to know. 'I'm an accountant by profession but found the job too restrictive. I completed a degree in psychology for kicks, anything to break out of the staid accountancy mould. And here I am, trying to combine the two.'

He fixed her with yet another piercing stare. 'So what was so restrictive?'

'Everything,' she answered too quickly, before composing herself. 'I mean, some people just aren't cut out for that type of work and I'm one of them.'

He quirked an eyebrow. 'Why?'

'I like to live outside the box. I'll try anything once and being an accountant, surrounded by conservative types who try their utmost to stay inside that box, just didn't do it for me.' The interview had taken a decidedly personal turn and, rather than being insulted, Fleur was strangely flattered that he wanted to know what made her tick.

'Anything, huh?' He leaned towards her and for one, insane moment she thought he might kiss her.

She nodded, wondering if she'd lost her mind and mentally cursing Liv for filling her head with romantic notions from those damn novels she read.

He stood up and extended his hand. 'Good. In that case, you're hired.'

Fleur managed a smile as she placed her hand in his, more prepared this time for the little jolt of electricity that shot up her arm. 'Thanks for the opportunity. I won't let you down.'

She wasn't sure if he held her hand a fraction too long before dropping it. 'How soon can you start?'

'Whenever you want me.'

'Tonight?' And just like that, the air around them seemed to crackle with some indefinable force, leaving Fleur with the distinct urge to test the boundaries with her new boss.

So what if he acted as if he'd just stepped off the ark? Maybe she could help him lighten up a little and have some fun in the process.

But he's your boss.

The thought dampened her impish side in a second. What was she thinking?

She'd just landed a prime job with a large company that could set her own business on its way and what was she planning? To seduce the boss! She needed to get a life. Fast.

'Tonight is fine. What did you have in mind?'

He turned away from her and returned to the sanctuary of his desk. 'Why don't we have dinner and I can fill you in on the company?' Several papers were picked up and reshuffled, as if he didn't care about her answer.

Fleur's heart lurched at the thought of spending an evening with this man, who had the power to unnerve her without trying. 'Sure. Name the place and time.'

He looked up, an expression of relief softening his hard features. 'The Potter Lounge. At eight?'

Fleur hoped the surprise didn't show on her face. He'd just named one of Melbourne's stuffiest, pretentious restaurants, usually reserved for regular guests or those hell-bent on making an impression.

'Formal or cocktail wear?'

'Whatever takes your fancy.' His gaze wandered down the length of her body, leaving a trail of goose pimples in its wake. 'Though I'm sure you'd look great in anything.'

Heat flooded her cheeks, though before she could come up with an appropriate retort he stalked across the room and held the door open for her in an obvious sign of dismissal. 'See you tonight?'

Clutching her portfolio under one arm and swinging her handbag over the other, Fleur strode past him. 'See you then. And thanks once again for the opportunity, Mr Howard.'

'It's Darcy, remember?'

She managed a polite smile and nod before he shut the door.

It's Darcy, remember?

His deep voice echoed through her mind along with every word he'd uttered in her bizarre interview. After the impression he'd just made on her, how could she forget?

CHAPTER TWO

IT HAD been a long time since Darcy had taken a woman out for dinner. His ever-increasing schedule put paid to any social life he'd once had, not that any woman had held his interest long enough for him to consider pursuing her.

Until now.

He shook his head, mentally chastising himself for allowing his thoughts to head down that track. Fleur Adams was business, not pleasure, a fact he shouldn't forget if he wanted his company to survive.

So what if he'd already decided to hire her before the interview? He'd needed to know more about the woman who held the future of his business in her hands, besides the basics. In a way, that was what tonight would be also, another 'get to know you' session.

So was that why he'd picked the fanciest place to dine in town? They had to eat and he'd sooner indulge his passion for fine food and wine at a recognised establishment than some poor imitation. God, he sounded like a pompous ass at times! He would frighten the poor woman off if he spoke like that.

Funnily enough, he already had the impression that Fleur thought he was an old fuddy-duddy; that was why he'd paid her a compliment, in the hope she would realise that he wasn't above admiring a beautiful woman when he saw one, though her reaction had intrigued him. Young women these days rarely blushed and he wondered if her feisty words about 'trying anything once' were merely a front of false bravado too.

Maybe he could test her out? *And maybe you need your head read!*

Pulling up in front of the restaurant, he handed the car keys to the valet and almost bounced up the marble steps. Whoever had invented that stupid rule about not mixing business with pleasure? Tonight, he had every intention of pushing the boundaries.

Fleur took a steadying breath, tilted her chin up and walked into the elaborate dining room of the Potter Lounge, trying not to gawk. Muted chandeliers cast a soft glow on the antique furnishings and reflected off the polished silverware, creating a warm and inviting ambiance, while the crystal wineglasses shone in the flickering candlelight.

So much for keeping her imagination grounded. This place was built for romance, not business, and she had no idea why Darcy had suggested it.

Feeling self-conscious and hoping it didn't show, she allowed the *maître d'* to guide her to their table. Not just any table, it happened to be the cosiest one set in the furthest corner of the room and shielded from prying eyes by an exquisite hand-painted Japanese screen.

'Great,' she muttered under her breath, knowing that spending an evening dining with her handsome new boss had just taken on a whole new meaning—in her own head.

To make matters worse, Darcy stood up as she neared the table and her heart did that weird, somersault thing it had when they first met at the café. It had nothing to do with his clothes; he'd gone for the conservative look once again with a dark designer suit, white shirt and striped tie. However, the man inside the clothes exuded some powerful brand of pheromones that called to her; she hadn't experienced such a strong attraction in ages—if she was completely honest, probably never.

He pulled her seat out for her, a quaint, old-fashioned gesture that made her feel ultra-feminine. 'You look beautiful,' he murmured close to her ear as she sat down, raising her pulse another notch.

'Thanks.' To her annoyance, she felt heat creeping up her neck towards her cheeks. What was wrong with her? She *never* blushed, especially not when men paid her compliments.

'So you decided to go with cocktail attire, huh?'

'When in doubt, stick with the LBD.'

He raised an eyebrow. 'LBD?'

Was he kidding? Surely he couldn't be *that* old?

Fleur grinned, a knowing smile that put her back on the front foot again and restored her confidence no end. 'Little black dress. The essential of every female's wardrobe.'

'Ah,' he said and nodded, as if he knew exactly what she was referring to, though by the confused look on his face, he had no idea.

'I thought a man like you would be used to dining with a host of women in LBDs,' she teased, hoping to lighten the mood.

'No time.' He gestured to a waiter hovering nearby and placed an order for champagne—of the French kind.

Something about his assumption that she drank expensive champagne or should be impressed by it grated on her nerves before she reminded herself of the purpose of the night. 'Tell me about your company. I don't even know what you import,' she said.

'Gift ware, mostly.'

'There's a huge market for that type of product. Why isn't the company turning a profit?'

He shook his head. 'If I knew the answer to that, I wouldn't need to hire you.'

Her eyebrows shot heavenward at his bitter tone.

'What I meant to say was my staff aren't as productive as they once were. Everyone seems to be infected with this strange kind of lethargy and, despite our trying a few things, nothing has shaken them out of it.'

Fleur remembered the receptionist and her cavalier attitude and knew exactly what he referred to.

'They used to have fun when they came to work but not any more.'

Suddenly, an image of Darcy's stodgy office popped into her mind. 'Do *you* have fun at work?'

He stared at her as if she'd spoken in some foreign language. 'What do you mean?'

She sipped at her recently filled flute and savoured the tingle of bubbles sliding down her throat. 'You know, the F word that people are scared to acknowledge at work. Is your work *fun*?'

'Work is work. If I wanted to have fun, I'd employ a bunch of clowns.'

'Well, maybe that's what you need to do.'

He rubbed the bridge of his nose while she sipped at her champagne, as if what she'd said pained him. 'Are you out of your mind?'

She sat up, suddenly businesslike. 'No, but I'd like to plant some ideas in yours.'

She took a deep breath and hoped her new boss was ready to hear the truth. 'OK, listen up. First impressions of your company are, quite frankly, that it's tame, bland and boring. From the reception area to the furniture, I think you need a major overhaul. Urgently.'

Rather than appearing angry, he leaned forward and rested his forearms on the table. 'So, you think I'm boring?'

'I was referring to your company.' For the life of her, she couldn't figure out which demon prompted her to add, 'I don't know enough about you yet to make that sort of judgement call.'

He ignored her jibe. 'Tell me more.'

'Most employees need to feel valued but, more importantly, they need to care enough about their job to want to excel at it.' She paused to tuck a stray strand of hair behind her ear, wondering if she had the courage to say exactly what she thought the problem was. 'From first impressions, I don't think your staff feel that way.'

'Why?' A frown creased his brow, adding five years onto his age and reinforcing what she was about to say.

She took several unladylike gulps of champagne, needing every ounce of fortitude she could muster. 'Bottom line? They're taking their cue from you.'

His frown deepened and she resisted the impulse to sink into her chair—or, better yet, slide under the table and slink out of the fancy restaurant. 'What's that supposed to mean?'

She exhaled, unaware she'd been holding her breath. 'Well, you seem to be a bit stuck yourself.'

'Stuck?' His eyebrows shot upward and, if she wasn't treading on such delicate ground, she would've laughed at his comical expression.

Crossing her fingers beneath the tablecloth, she continued and hoped to God she still had a job by the end of this. 'You intimidate people. The way you look, the way you dress, how you carry yourself, all screams ''unapproachable''. And if *you* don't enjoy your work, how do you expect your staff to?'

She waited for the explosion. Heck, she would've given him a verbal spray if he'd had the audacity to tell her all that to her face after only one meeting. Instead, he leaned back, folded his arms and fixed her with a glare.

'I can see where that psychology degree comes in handy. Now that you've analysed me and the company, how do you propose to sort the problem out?'

She quelled the nervous flutter within her gut. Whenever he looked at her like that, she couldn't think straight. Something about the deep blue of his eyes had her focusing on all the wrong cues, starting with how she could lose herself in their depths.

'That's easy.' She managed a smile, hoping it didn't look more like a grimace. 'We start at the top and work our way down.'

'Now, that sounds like an interesting proposition.' His eyes brightened with an almost imperceptible gleam which she recognised as interest and her heart thudded in response. For someone who appeared stuffy at first glance, he sure knew how to turn innocent words into innuendo.

'I'd prefer to think of it as challenging. After all, you don't strike me as the type of man who takes to change very well.'

'I'm that easy to read, huh?' He leaned forward, the simple act lending an immediate intimacy to the moment.

'Call it intuition.' She picked up the menu, needing to do something with her fiddling hands and distract her attention from his probing gaze.

To her amazement, he reached across the table and plucked the menu from her hands. 'Let's finish this discussion before we order. What needs to be done to turn this situation around?'

I need to run a thousand miles away from you and those damn eyes.

Maybe taking this job hadn't been such a good idea! Sure, she was desperate for business, not to mention that wonderful commodity that made the world go round, but was it worth feeling this flustered, this unsure of herself? She'd never lacked confidence, therefore this guy's ability to undermine her with a single glance was more than disconcerting. It was downright frightening.

'How about I present a business plan to you over the next few days and we take it from there?'

'But you mentioned starting at the top. I assume you meant with me.'

She nodded. 'I have a few ideas but I'd like to interview some of your staff to get a general feel for the place before I present my plan. That's how I usually work.' A small white lie but she had no intention of letting him know this was her first real assignment. Besides, she'd honed her own business plan to the nth degree and knew she could handle anything her new boss had to dish out. Within reason.

'Fine.' He handed her the menu. 'I look forward to hearing this master plan of yours.'

She sighed in relief, though it was short-lived.

'Just remember, Fleur. I'm expecting big things from you. And I don't like to be let down.'

'You don't need to worry,' she said, knowing that she'd be doing enough of that for the both of them.

Darcy turned the key in the lock, surprised to find the front door to his house open. He could've sworn he'd locked it when he left earlier that evening. Maybe the thought of having dinner with Fleur had rattled him more than he'd anticipated?

However, as he entered the house and heard the pounding bass reverberating through the hallway, he knew why the door was unlocked.

He took the stairs two at a time, torn between wanting to hug his wayward brother and throttle him for being away so long. Sean's bedroom door stood open, explaining the ear-splitting noise from some heavy-metal band Darcy had probably never heard of.

'Hey, bro; long time, no see.' Sean jumped up from the bed, piece of pizza in one hand and a beer in the other, a wide grin plastered across his face.

Darcy turned down the volume before answering. 'Is that what you call three years? A long time?'

Sean's smile slipped a notch. 'Come on, man. Don't be so...parental. Aren't you glad to see me?'

The familiar anger surged through Darcy's body, rooting him to the spot. He'd raised Sean from the age of eleven yet the passing years hadn't instilled maturity into his brother. Sean had never recognised the sacrifices Darcy had made in raising him, preferring to see him as some sort of ogre rather than a caring brother who'd been thrust into the role of parent at too young an age.

If anything, Sean still lived the life of a carefree boy and it irked Darcy more than it should. Why should he be the one to always shoulder all the responsibility? Now that his brother was thirty years old, surely it was time he started acting like it?

'Two phone calls in three years. Don't you think I've earned the right to be concerned?'

Sean shook his head and took a swig from his beer. 'I can see you haven't changed much.'

'Neither have you.' Darcy clenched his fists, surprised that the years away hadn't matured his brother. He still spoke and behaved like a wayward teenager, from his smart mouth to his taste in music. 'So, how long are you staying around this time?'

Sean shrugged, as if he didn't have a care in the world. 'Who knows? I might hang out here for a while, see what Melbourne has to offer these days.'

'How's the cash situation?' Darcy resisted the urge to cringe; as much as he tried, he couldn't shake the role of a worried father, probing his son for scraps of information about his life. He knew Sean didn't like it and he sure as hell wished he could stop it. However, it had been a habit for almost twenty years and he'd be damned if he stopped caring now.

'Stop worrying, bro. Is it any wonder you've got grey hairs?'

'I have not!'

'Sure you have. You've got one, right about there.' Sean threw the pizza crust back in the cardboard box and walked towards him, pointing to Darcy's temple. 'Yep, I see it. Actually, it's more white than grey.'

'Brat!' Darcy swatted Sean's hand away and finally smiled, allowing a glimmer of affection to show in his eyes.

'Yeah, I've missed you too, bro.' Sean enveloped him in a bear hug and Darcy returned it, slapping his brother on the back.

Once they'd broken apart and looked away, unsure how to break that awkward pause that inevitably accompanied men embracing each other, Darcy headed towards the door. He stopped on the threshold and looked back, happier than he'd been in a long time. 'It's good to have you home, Sean.'

Sean grinned, the same cheeky grin he'd had as an eleven-year-old. 'Good to be back, even if I have to look at your ugly mug!'

Darcy pulled a face and turned away, wondering what Fleur would think if she could see him now. He'd managed to forget about their interesting evening once he'd entered the house, though the memory of her now resurfaced.

She'd looked incredible in that black dress with the neckline cut high enough to be classy yet low enough to entice. He'd been impressed, from her sleek hair—it must've taken her at least an hour to straighten those gorgeous curls he'd admired when they first met—to her sequined sandals and everything in between. In fact, he'd had a hard time keeping his mind on the conversation when his attention kept wandering to the 'everything in between'.

Though he had gained one pertinent fact. The lady thought he couldn't lighten up.

Well, he would show her.

CHAPTER THREE

THANKS to her psychology background, Fleur always analysed any date with a male, from the way he'd looked at her to what he'd said, and unfortunately her date with Darcy sent her analytical brain into overtime.

Date? Where had that come from? He'd taken her on a business dinner, not a date, and the sooner she remembered that the better.

So what if he'd plied her with fine food and wine, asking personal questions to appear as if he was genuinely interested in her? She knew what he'd been playing at—any boss worth his weight would interrogate a new employee like that, especially one who was investing so much time and money into saving his ailing company.

It wasn't his fault that her overactive imagination had taken flight and read more into it. Despite her best intentions to appear professional, her guard had slipped several times and she'd actually found herself responding to him like a woman, not an employee. Not that he hadn't encouraged her a tad; she could've sworn she glimpsed desire in his eyes several times, and each time her body had betrayed her with a hot rush of anticipation that still left her slightly breathless.

Thankfully, she hadn't seen much of him since dinner two nights ago. Whenever she'd been interviewing his employees, he'd been holed up in his dreary office or off on some buying expedition, giving her free rein within the office and some control over her peace of mind.

However, she'd known it wouldn't last and today she had to present her completed business plan to him, a situation which should've thrilled her yet didn't. She'd done a thorough job and should be proud of herself—however, how did she tell him the truth without denting the man's ego in the process? Or worse yet, stirring his wrath to the point where he might fire her?

She'd dressed to impress, knowing that presenting a front would be the first step in calming her nerves. However, the minute she walked into Darcy's office and he looked up at her with that all-seeing stare, she wished she'd chosen something more conservative than the bottle-green skirt that skimmed her knees and the matching jacket which gave a glimpse of black camisole underneath.

'Coffee?' he offered.

She shook her head—she was wired up enough already!

'How's the plan looking?' He gestured towards the uncomfortable seat and she knew that would be the first piece of furniture to go.

'All done.' She resisted the urge to tug her skirt down as she sat, knowing he watched her every move.

He sat back, a smirk playing around the corners of his mouth. 'Let me have it.'

She stared at his lips, wondering how she could've judged them as being thin that first day they'd met in the café. He had great lips and the longer she stared at them, the more curious she became to know exactly how they might feel plastered against hers.

He leaned forward and reached out for the cup of coffee on the desk in front of him, allowing her valuable time to recompose herself whilst he took a sip. So much for playing it cool. Focusing on his lips had set her body on fire and she hoped her raised temperature didn't reflect in her fiery cheeks.

She cleared her throat. 'Before I present this, I need to know if you're ready.'

'Ready and raring.' He smiled, sending her heart hammering as she glimpsed a spark of desire in his eyes.

Looking at the documents in her hands, which shook slightly as she rearranged the papers for the hundredth time since they'd come off the printer that morning, she wrenched her attention back to the task at hand. 'I've prepared this plan with one aim in mind and that's to get your business back on track, as you requested. In doing this, I've spent time with most of your staff, who are more than loyal, yet I managed to read between the lines.'

'Oh?' The smile faded, only to be re-placed by the frown that intimidated her.

Quelling her nerves with effort, she continued. 'Your team have a genuine love of their jobs, they have a shared pur-pose and trust in the company's mission statement and are keen to see progression within the organisation.'

'But?'

Trying to stall for time, she placed the documents on the desk and clasped her hands in her lap, wishing he wasn't so darn intuitive. She'd given him all the positives first, yet, being an astute businessman, he'd known she'd left the most important information out.

'It's not enough.' She looked away and focused her attention on the dull picture behind him, of a sailing ship battling murky waters. Yet another indication that this dreary office needed an overhaul.

'Tell me, Fleur. I want to hear it all.'

She braced herself for a possible eruption and stared him straight in the eye. 'You've lost your spark. I get the feeling that your employees are having a hard time appearing interested in their work when the boss walks in here every day and looks like he's shouldering the weight of the world.'

He ran a finger around the inside of his collar, as if her statement along with his tie were choking him. 'Continue.'

'Though they didn't say it in as many words, I knew what they were implying.

It's difficult to appear perky when *you* trudge in here as if it's the last place you want to be.' She spoke in a rush, trying to get the words out in a hurry and thus prevent him from interrupting and shredding the last of her resolve to tell him the truth. 'And it isn't just your attitude. Take this office, for instance.' She gestured around her. 'It's dull and lifeless. Anyone who sets foot in here would want to escape ASAP.' She wriggled back in her seat as if to prove a point. 'Me included. I hate this chair!'

'Are you quite finished?'

She flushed, his icy tone scaring her more than she cared to admit. 'Here. It's all documented.'

He took the report from her and threw it on his desk, adding it to the growing pile of paperwork already stashed in his in-tray. 'I'll read it later. So, now that you've discovered the problem, what's the solution?'

He planted his hands on the desk and towered over her, the thunderous look on his face intimidating her more than the quietly controlled fury in his voice.

'I teach you how to have fun.'

Darcy sat down in his chair again, stunned by Fleur's solution to his business problems. She stared at him with those wide chocolate-brown eyes without blinking and, with a jolt, he realised she was serious.

He laughed, a bitter sound that echoed through the room. 'You're kidding, right? *You* want to teach *me* how to have fun?'

'That's right.' She nodded, almost dislodging the weird bun arrangement perched precariously on top of her head. He preferred her hair loose and swinging across her shoulders the way she'd worn it at dinner or, better yet, curling seductively around her face like the first memorable time he'd seen her.

'Let me get this straight. I need to *learn* how to have fun?'

She blushed again and he had a strong urge to reach across the desk and cup her cheek in his hand. 'More like you need to loosen up and remember what it was like, perhaps?'

He stifled a grin. Though she hadn't told him anything he didn't already know, he'd been surprised that his employees felt that way about him. He knew he'd lost his spark, feeling as if he was just going through the motions most days. He wished he could be more like Sean, able to shun his responsibilities and travel the world in search of the next best thing. But he couldn't. He'd seen his father do that and look how that had ended, with both his parents dead in the process.

So he trudged along, throwing himself into his work yet knowing that he'd become more and more introverted along the way. He rarely socialised, dated or went out any more, unless it pertained to business, and it obviously showed. All work and no play had definitely made him a dull boy—with a woman like Fleur around, maybe it was time to change all that?

'OK, let's say for argument's sake that you're right. How are you going to get me to loosen up?' Darcy couldn't wait to hear this.

She fiddled with the top button on her jacket, drawing his attention to the hint of black camisole underneath. And just like that, Darcy knew exactly how his delicious new employee could help him loosen up while simultaneously chastising himself for fantasising about the unattainable.

For that was what Fleur was—he couldn't dare let himself get close to her, for she was the epitome of every characteristic he'd schooled himself to avoid: brash, daring to be different, needing to break out of a mould. She was just like Sean and his father and he'd be damned if he ended up like them. Living for the moment ended in pain and he'd learned to block out anything—or anyone—that could instigate that emotion.

'You need to have fun. I'm going to show you the ropes.' She stood and gathered her bag and laptop. 'Meet me out the front of this building at eight tomorrow morning. And wear something casual.'

He watched her stride towards the door, admiring her slim legs and the way her skirt hugged her butt, wondering how both would feel beneath his hands.

'But tomorrow's Saturday,' he said, wondering if she thought he was such a sad case that they needed to get started on her plan immediately.

She stopped, hand poised on the door-knob. 'So? Or would you prefer to start tonight?'

He glimpsed the challenge in her eyes, curious to know more and ready to face what she had in mind. 'The sooner the better.'

'Fine. I'll pick you up at ten tonight. And the same dress code applies.'

Ten? As in two hours before midnight? He was usually falling asleep at that time rather than heading out.

He saw her look of triumph and quickly masked his surprise. He wouldn't give her the satisfaction of asking what she had planned at that hour. 'See you then. It's 20, The Terrace, South Yarra.'

'No problem.' She opened the door and stepped through it, leaving him burning with curiosity.

Liv lay sprawled on Fleur's bed as she dressed, bombarding her with a host of questions she'd rather not answer.

'He took you to dinner at the Potter Lounge and now you're taking him to a nightclub. Doesn't that constitute dating the boss, not working for him?'

Fleur fastened her earrings and glared at Liv's reflection in the mirror. 'Give it a rest, will you? I'm working tonight, not socialising.'

Liv snorted. 'Yeah, right. Nice outfit for *working*.'

'We're going clubbing. I had to wear something like this.' She smoothed the fabric over her hips, knowing that the skintight black trousers and matching halter-neck top would be viewed as conservative by most of the patrons at the club she'd planned on taking Darcy to.

'I wish I had a job like yours, smooching up to the likes of that hunky boss. Girl, I don't know how you do it but the good ones always seem to fall into your lap.'

Good ones? Fleur could barely remember the last time she'd met a nice guy, one who wasn't just interested in jumping into bed at the end of the first date.

Feigning a haughty look, Fleur twirled around to face her friend. 'Darcy didn't fall into my lap. My head connected with his elbow, remember?'

'Nice one. Maybe I should try that some time, though, knowing my luck, some jerk would spill his drink all over me rather than offering me a dream job.'

'Hey, this isn't a dream job. It's *a* job.'

Liv sat up. 'You're getting paid to spend time with a guy like Darcy and you get to teach him how to have fun, which draws up all sorts of interesting connotations.' She paused for a moment and scratched her head. 'Mmm…can't see why I'd think it was a dream job, can you?'

Fleur grinned and applied the finishing touches to her make-up. 'Point taken. Though what if I fail? In getting him to loosen up, that is?'

The thought had crossed her mind and, though she'd just made light of it with

Liv, it had worried her ever since she'd left his office today, brimming with false bravado.

'Easy. Seduce him.'

Fleur flung Ripley, her treasured stuffed puppy, at Liv's head. Her friend ducked and laughed, while Fleur determinedly ignored the surge of excitement that Liv's joking words conjured up.

Darcy paced the living room, watching the clock and feeling utterly ridiculous in the process.

'You're going out? At this hour?' Sean leaned against the doorframe, a grin spreading across his face.

'What's it to you?' Darcy almost growled, wishing he'd never agreed to Fleur picking him up. Though Sean had been out most of the time since he'd returned, he'd stayed home tonight, the one night that Darcy didn't want him here.

'Hey, just call it brotherly concern. Now, listen up. Don't stay out too late, don't drink too much and stay out of trouble.' Sean ticked the points off on his fingers, imitating the action and tone of countless lectures Darcy had dished out to him as a teenager. 'And ring me if you need me!'

'OK, wise guy. Enough.' He strode to the window and looked out, wondering if he could make a run for it as soon as Fleur pulled up outside.

Sean whistled. 'Wow, this chick must be something to get you this wound up. How long has it been since you had a date, anyway?'

'This isn't a date.' The words slipped out before Darcy had time to think and he mentally kicked himself.

'Then what is it?'

'None of your business.' Darcy glared at his brother, wishing he'd disappear.

Unfortunately, Sean had distracted him from watching for Fleur and the doorbell rang at that moment. Worse still, his brother sprinted for the door before he could move.

Stifling a groan, Darcy followed Sean and watched with growing trepidation as he opened the front door.

'Hi, I'm Fleur. Is Darcy here?'

Darcy stopped dead in the hallway, several paces behind Sean and hidden by an antique grandfather clock. He stared at Fleur in disbelief, floored by the sultry temptress she'd become.

Sure, he'd already admired her great figure but the body she displayed tonight should have a warning slapped all over it—'Dangerous Curves Ahead'. It looked as if she'd been poured into her outfit and his palms itched to smooth over every inch of her. She'd used make-up to high-light her eyes and lips, lending them an exotic quality that beckoned like a siren, and she'd done something wild to her hair, which framed her face in corkscrew curls. Stunning would barely come close to describing how she looked and she was all his…well, at least for the length of her contract, though work was the fur-thest thing from his mind at this point.

Sean opened the door wider. 'Yeah, my old fogey of a brother's here. I'm Sean, by the way. *Very* pleased to meet you.'

Darcy resisted the urge to strangle Sean as his brother planted a kiss on the back of Fleur's hand.

Her eyes sparkled as she looked up at Sean and Darcy wished she would look at him like that, even once. 'Nice to meet you.'

'Pretty name for a pretty lady. French for flower. I like that.' Sean hadn't changed a bit; he'd always laid it on thick when it came to the ladies and Darcy felt like throwing up.

'Thanks, but I'm no shrinking violet.'

Darcy smiled—that was his Fleur, full of sass.

His Fleur? Where had that come from?

He walked towards the door, keen to leave his smooth-talking brother behind and get this mystery evening underway.

'Hi, Fleur. Ready to go?'

Her gaze flicked over him and, thankfully, he read approval in her eyes. 'Sure, let's hit the road.'

Sean slapped him on the back. 'Have fun, you two. Don't do anything I wouldn't do.' He blew a kiss at Fleur, who captured it in her hand, placed it on her cheek and winked.

'Don't encourage him,' Darcy muttered, almost dragging her down the path towards her car.

'He's harmless,' she said, unlocking the car with a stab at the remote on her key ring.

'Yeah, if you like sharks.'

She laughed as she slid into the seat and started the engine. 'This evening's about lightening up, remember?'

'I'll try.' He glanced out the window as the car shot away from the kerb, trying to ignore the way her hand confidently handled the gear stick and the responding reaction in his groin as his mind shifted into fantasy mode.

'I didn't know you had a brother,' Fleur commented.

'There's a lot you don't know about me.'

Starting with how much I'd like to kiss you right now.

'Why don't you tell me something about yourself?' She geared down as they neared traffic lights and he shifted uncomfortably in his seat.

'Might be too *boring* for you.'

'I'm willing to take the risk if you are.'

Though her tone was flippant, Darcy knew their conversation had taken an unexpected twist and he decided to notch the heat up a little.

'As of now, consider risk to be my middle name.'

The car slowed to a halt at the red light and she turned to face him, an impish smile tugging at the corners of her glossed mouth. 'Maybe there's hope for you yet.'

'Don't write me off as a lost cause too soon. I might surprise you.' *With a little bit of luck.*

Her eyes glowed in the dimness and for a moment he wished he had the power to light up her eyes like that all the time. 'I just love surprises.'

Correction; make that a *lot* of luck. Who was he trying to kid? It had been a long time since he'd been out with a woman, let alone brought a sparkle to her eyes. And as for surprising her, he had a better chance of impressing her with his trivia knowledge than stunning her with his spontaneous personality!

He wrenched his gaze away from hers with an effort and stared straight ahead. 'I think green means go.'

She laughed and floored it, screeching away from the traffic lights in a cloud of smoke.

He gripped the dashboard and cast her a look that would have intimidated most women. Predictably, it had little effect on her as she quirked an eyebrow and sent him a cocky grin before returning her attention to the road.

'You didn't tell me that rally driving was one of your hidden talents.'

Her grin widened. 'You're not the only one who has secrets, you know. I'll show you mine if you show me yours.'

Her innuendo had him focusing on all the wrong cues, like her delicious scent filling the car and infusing his senses, the way her hands handled the steering wheel with consummate ease, the tight fit of her trousers outlining a lean thigh. He hadn't been this attracted to a woman in ages—hell, had any woman ever turned him on this much?

She was his employee, for goodness' sake, and he'd better start remembering it before he made a complete ass of himself. 'How about we start by you telling me where we're going tonight, at this hour?'

'You don't get out much, do you?'

He grimaced, thankful that she couldn't see the expression on his face now that she was finally concentrating on the road. 'I get around.'

'Oh, yeah?'

'Yeah.' He injected as much confidence as he could muster into his answer, knowing it wouldn't fool her for a second.

It didn't. 'Tell me, then, where does a guy like you go *at this hour* for kicks?'

She knew, dammit, she knew that he was a fraud. He rarely started an evening after ten; in fact, most of his outings were winding down at this time, a fact he had no intention of telling her. She'd had enough laughs at his expense already.

'I like the finer things in life.'

She chuckled. 'You didn't answer my question.'

'When I go out, it's usually to art galleries, wine tastings, things like that...' He trailed off, wondering when his favourite activities had started sounding so dull.

'Well, la-di-da.' She pulled into a narrow side-street and brought the car to a halt, without burning rubber this time. 'In that case, you'd better keep an open mind about tonight. Where I'm taking you, there isn't a picture or sculpture in sight.'

He cast a quick glance around, noting they'd entered the seedier part of Melbourne, the dimly lit streets lined with nightclubs and girlie bars. 'I'm in your hands,' he said, suddenly wishing it were true, literally.

'Lucky me.' Her smile sent his blood pressure soaring and his imagination into overdrive. 'Let's get lesson number one underway.'

CHAPTER FOUR

'Do YOU come here often?'

Fleur jumped and whirled around, ready to put the jerk that had whispered the pathetic line in her ear firmly back in his place. 'Oh, it's you,' she said, stifling a grin as Darcy handed her a drink.

'Well, do you?' He clinked glasses with her and she wondered if the clear liquid he sipped was vodka or water. Knowing the type of guy he was, she assumed it was the latter.

'Time you got a new line. That one doesn't work with the ladies any more. In fact, it went out about the same time as disco balls and bubble skirts.'

'It wasn't a line. I just wondered if you did this sort of thing all the time. For *fun.*' He gestured towards the dance floor, packed with writhing bodies gyrating to the latest techno beat.

She smiled at his bemused expression as two girls wearing hot pants and bikini tops pressed against each other, flinging their arms around each other in total abandon while a group of guys cheered them on. 'I've been here a few times.'

'So what do you do, apart from *that*?' He pointed towards the dance floor and grimaced, as if the dancers were some sort of alien life form.

'Have you ever tried *that*?' She asked provocatively, unable to imagine him dancing to anything other than his parents' Frank Sinatra ballads and instilling the right amount of scepticism into her voice in the hope he'd take the bait.

Typical of any male she'd ever challenged, he did.

'No, but how hard can it be? Let's go.' He grabbed her hand and dragged her towards the dance floor, barely giving her time to place her empty glass on a nearby table.

'Settle down, John Travolta,' she muttered as he pushed through the crowd and headed for the middle of the dance floor.

OK, so maybe she should've thought this little scenario through before issuing her challenge, for she hadn't banked on her body being plastered against his as the throng jostled them from all sides.

'See, there's nothing to it,' he whispered in her ear as his hips moulded to hers, sending desire shooting through her body.

'Pardon?' She pretended not to hear him above the deafening beat, knowing he'd have to speak into her ear again. The feel of his warm breath against her earlobe the first time around had sent shivers down her spine and she wanted to experience it all over again.

In response, he pulled her closer if that was possible, their proximity forcing her to wrap her hands around his neck and hang on. His body pressed against her and she revelled in every inch of contact, wishing the barrier of their clothing would suddenly disappear, leaving them in an intimate embrace of skin on skin.

'Now, *this* is fun.' He gyrated in time with the music, his sense of rhythm surprising her—though it had nothing on the surprise waiting for her as she shifted her pelvis slightly and met the hard evidence of exactly how much fun he was having.

She should've been flattered that she'd aroused him. Heck, she should've been doing cartwheels, for it meant that she wasn't the only one caught up in this

weird attraction that until now she
thought she'd conjured up in her mind.
However, to her amazement, she suddenly blushed, overcome by an intense
shyness that left her wanting to run from
the club.

Unable to meet his eyes, she pulled
away. 'End of lesson number one,' she
yelled above the throbbing bass. 'Time
for a break.'

He nodded and followed her off the
dance floor, not speaking till they'd
reached the quieter area near the bar. 'I
was just getting warmed up. How did I
do?'

His eyes glittered in the fluorescent
lights, making it impossible for her to
gauge if he was teasing or serious. She
stepped away, anxious to put as much
distance as possible between them before

she did something stupid like lean into him again.

'Not bad for a novice.' She kept her response deliberately cool in the hope he wouldn't see how much he'd rattled her.

'What does lesson two entail?' He reached out and wound a curl around his finger, tugging her towards him.

Her breath hitched as he drew her closer and she struggled to concentrate on the words that formed in her brain but didn't quite reach her mouth. 'Maybe it's best if we save the next lesson till tomorrow?'

'Don't be *boring*,' he whispered wickedly against the corner of her mouth a split-second before he slanted his lips across hers.

Fleur had been kissed before, but not like this. His lips were soft yet in total command, delivering a slow, lingering kiss that rendered her powerless to do anything but melt into it. The logical part of her brain kept flashing warning signals that being kissed by her boss was wrong—very wrong—while her body happily ignored it and threw itself whole-heartedly into returning his kiss.

She closed her eyes and leaned into him, savouring the feel of his hands skimming her back, burning a trail through the flimsy material of her top. He deepened the kiss and she responded on an intuitive level, wishing his hot mouth could wreak the same havoc on the rest of her body as she gave herself over to experiencing the touch of a master.

When he finally lifted his mouth a fraction from hers she could barely breathe, let alone talk.

'That was good,' he murmured, tracing a slow line down her cheek with his fingertip. 'Very good.'

To her horror, her throat tightened with emotion and she couldn't think of one witty thing to say to lighten the moment. Usually she'd laugh off these situations, but not tonight. Darcy had undermined her confidence on a deeper level and she definitely didn't want to go there. Not now, not ever. She had no aspirations to find a man and settle down, as Liv did. Her parents' marriage had ruined that little fantasy forever.

'Are you OK?' He stepped away from her, concern evident in the set of his shoulders, the lines around his eyes.

Taking a deep breath, Fleur fixed a smile on her face. 'Sure. You're a fast learner. At this rate, you'll be having fun in no time at all.'

He ran a hand through his hair, looking thoroughly rattled. 'Look, about that kiss—'

'No problem. You needed to show the teacher how quickly you're progressing and I'm impressed.' If only he knew just how good his technique was! 'Very impressed.'

His face relaxed into the semblance of a smile. 'I'll take that as a compliment.'

'You should.'

Suddenly the atmosphere around them heated up again, but before he could respond someone wrapped their hands around her eyes from behind.

'Guess who, gorgeous?'

Fleur stifled a groan. Of all the people she would've liked to avoid tonight, her ex would be number one on the list. 'Hi, Mitch. How are you?'

Mitch dropped his hands and spun her around, enveloping her in a hug. 'Great...now that you're here.' He leaned closer and whispered in her ear. 'Who's Grandad?'

Fleur pulled away and resisted the urge to slap him. 'Darcy, I'd like you to meet Mitch, an old friend of mine.'

'Hey, dude.' Mitch shook Darcy's hand and Fleur almost cringed.

Dude? Had he always spoken like that when she'd been with him? If so, her taste in men was worse than she thought, though being attracted to Darcy meant her judgement was undergoing a vast improvement.

'Nice to meet you,' Darcy said, looking anything but pleased at meeting Mitch.

'Fancy a dance?' Mitch draped his arm across her shoulders as if he owned her.

She shrugged out of it. 'No, thanks. We were just leaving.'

'Past your bedtime, huh?' He stared at Darcy and Fleur knew what he was implying. Was the age difference that obvious? She'd placed Darcy in his mid-thirties and thought that he looked younger tonight, dressed in casual black trousers and an open-necked white shirt rather than his usual suits. However, by the amused look on Mitch's face, he thought Darcy was over the hill.

As she opened her mouth to come back with a scathing reply, Darcy answered, 'Actually, you're right, mate. With a woman like this by my side, can't blame a guy for thinking along those lines.' To her amazement, he grabbed hold of her hand, flashed a dazzling smile at Mitch and walked away, leaving her little choice but to follow.

Fleur waited till they were outside before yanking her hand out of his. 'What was that all about?'

'What?' His innocent act didn't fool her for a second.

'That macho rubbish you pulled back there before dragging me out like a caveman.' Though she'd never admit it to him, a small part of her had been impressed by how he'd dealt with that jerk Mitch.

He had the grace to look sheepish. 'Sorry, you didn't deserve that. It's just that your boyfriend made me feel ancient and I wanted to put him back in his place.'

'How did you know he was a boyfriend?'

'I may be old but I'm not blind or stupid. He acted like he owned you.'

'He wishes!' She'd hated the way Mitch behaved when they'd been together and, by the looks of it, not much had changed. He still thought he'd been put on this earth to make women happy though, in her case, miserable had been more like it.

She shook her head. 'I can't stand guys who act like that. He couldn't take it slow if he tried; always pushing for...' She trailed off, doubting that Darcy would want to hear about Mitch's antics to coerce her into the bedroom.

'Come on, let's go. I've had enough lessons for one night,' he said, sounding surprisingly bitter and unable to meet her eye.

Fleur raised an eyebrow, not quite understanding where his tone was coming from. Surely he realised she was angry with Mitch, not him? However, he'd turned away and drummed his fingers on the car, obviously impatient to end the evening.

Rolling her eyes and wishing a pox on the male species in general, she unlocked the car, slid behind the wheel and drove him home.

Darcy sipped his espresso and sighed, wondering how long it had been since he'd taken time out on a weekend to relax, have a coffee and read the newspaper. Too long, if his simple enjoyment in scanning the sports section was any indication.

'So, how did the big date go?' Sean stumbled into the kitchen, looking more bleary-eyed than usual.

'I thought you were staying in last night?' Darcy drained his mug and emphatically rustled the paper, in no mood for his brother's interrogation.

'Shh! Stop making such a racket. Oh, my aching head.' Sean massaged his temple while rummaging in a cupboard and coming up with aspirin.

'Big night, huh?' Darcy smirked and momentarily wondered why he felt so damn good for someone who'd got to bed at two a.m. after having his eardrums perforated by music designed to wake the dead.

'Last-minute plans. Went to a new club.' Sean swallowed the aspirin followed by an orange-juice chaser before drawing up a chair and leaning his head in his hands. 'I want details, bro. Now.'

'I had a good time.'

'I had a good time,' mimicked Sean in the plummiest tone he could muster. 'Come on, don't hold out on me. Fleur's a hottie. What is she doing spending time with you?'

Darcy smiled, determined not to let anything spoil his mood on this all-round great morning. 'Jealous, huh?' He turned a page and pretended to study the latest football results. 'Face it, little bro. Some of us have it, some of us don't.'

'Hey, I've got it. In spades!'

'And who told you that? The ladies or your own super-inflated ego?'

Suddenly, Sean lifted his head. 'I know what's got you so damned happy. You got some last night, didn't you?'

And just like that, Darcy's good mood evaporated and he wanted to beat his brother into a pulp for inferring that Fleur would be the kind of woman to sleep with him on a first date. Not that it had been a date, though he wouldn't waste his breath explaining the finer details to his Neanderthal brother.

'Leave it alone, Sean,' he said, hoping his icy tone would convince his brother to drop the subject.

Sean held up his hands in apparent surrender. 'Hey, take it easy, man. Not one to kiss and tell, huh?'

In response, Darcy stalked out of the kitchen and headed for the one place known to instil some degree of normality into his life—the office.

Fleur slunk into the back of the gym as the aerobics class started and breathed a sigh of relief. At least she would be saved from Liv's questions for the moment, though her luck would run out as soon as the class ended. She needed some breathing space—heck, she needed her head read after what had happened last night.

So much for teaching Darcy to loosen up and live a little. She'd been the one to learn a lesson and he'd played her like a pro, kissing her with the expertise of a man seasoned in the art of seduction.

She'd had it all planned: take him to a nightclub where he'd feel so out of place that he'd demand to leave and she could use his reticence to prove exactly how 'over the hill' he appeared to others. However, he'd surprised her and hadn't complained about the loud music, the way-out patrons or the dingy atmosphere as she'd expected. Instead they had danced, and had a scintillating kiss, two activities commonly seen and quite acceptable in that environment.

She inwardly groaned as she stretched during cool-down, wondering how long it had been since she'd been kissed in public at a nightclub. Probably high school! Even Mitch hadn't been that open, which was saying something.

Though the kiss had been meaningless, she wondered why someone as controlled as Darcy would lose his head for a moment and do something like that, in a place like that. Had he been teasing her or trying to turn the tables on her to prove a point? Either way, it had shaken her more than she cared to admit and she would need to stay on guard during the next few ventures she'd planned for him. Not that she thought he'd put in a repeat performance, though there was no telling what *she* might be prompted to do if they got that close again.

The sound of clapping hands roused her from her reverie and she realised the class had ended. As predicated, Liv made a beeline for her as Fleur attempted to sidle out the back door.

'Not so fast. How did it go last night?' Liv placed her arm across the door, effectively barring Fleur's escape.

'Good. Now, if you don't mind, I'd like to shower.' Fleur attempted to push past Liv's arm with little success.

'Just good, huh? Surely there's more to tell than that? After all, if I'd been out with a guy like dishy Darcy, well...' Liv wiggled her eyebrows suggestively and made loud smacking noises with her lips, looking utterly ridiculous in the process.

'The evening went better than planned and I'm conducting the second lesson next week. Is that enough?'

Liv shook her head. 'Not really. I expected details like, did he look hunky in what he wore, did he smell good, did you dance, did anything remotely romantic happen?'

Fleur grinned and decided to put her friend out of her misery. 'Yes, yes, yes and no.'

'No romance, huh?'

The memory of Darcy's lips brushing hers flashed through her mind, elevating her temperature higher than post-exercise levels as heat flooded her body. No, there'd been nothing romantic about that kiss. Scorching, yes. Romantic, well...

No! It had just been the circumstances pushing two people with a semi-attraction together. No big deal.

'Don't you ever quit?' Fleur said, wishing she could convince herself as easily. After she'd dropped Darcy home, she hadn't slept a wink, replaying every touch, every nuance, of their time together. Though exercise had been the last thing she felt like doing this morning, she'd needed something, anything, to take her mind off her boss and his amazing kissing technique.

Liv dropped her arm. 'OK, you win. But I'm not stupid. I know you're hiding something and I fully intend to find out what that is. Perhaps a latte and a muffin might do the trick?'

'Bribery will get you nowhere. My lips are sealed.' Fleur made a zipping action over her lips, knowing she should've done something similar last night.

At least that would've solved one problem, the one that had been bugging her ever since she'd dropped Darcy home.

How would she react if the situation arose again? And more importantly, would she react any differently?

CHAPTER FIVE

'IT'S been a week since lesson one. Are you ready for number two yet?' Fleur looked up from the spreadsheet she'd been perusing, impressed with the figures she'd seen so far.

'Is it going to be as much fun as lesson one was?' Darcy threw his pen onto the desk, clasped his fingers together and stretched.

She quirked an eyebrow. 'You're actually admitting that you had fun?'

'For some of the evening.' He stared at her, the intense blue of his eyes boring right through her and leaving her in little doubt as to what part of the evening he was referring to.

To her annoyance, she felt heat creep into her cheeks once more. How *did* he keep doing that to her? She was never bothered when guys flirted with her, so why start now?

Flirt? Is that what he's doing?

She met his gaze directly, no closer to figuring out her boss now than when she'd first met him. Usually, she prided herself on her ability to read people; it had been one of her strengths during her psychology degree. However, Darcy Howard had confounded her from day one and continued to do so, much to her chagrin.

'Lesson two will be more strenuous and a lot messier.'

His eyebrows shot heavenward. 'Sounds intriguing.'

'Oh, it is. And I bet it's something you've never done before.'

'You know, I can have fun. It involves going to museums, art galleries, wineries.'

'Bor-ing,' she answered, thinking that going to some of those places wouldn't be so boring if she had someone like Darcy to accompany her.

He shrugged, as if her opinion meant little. 'I wouldn't expect a young thing like you to understand sophisticated stuff like that.'

Though he was teasing, Fleur suddenly realised that the age gap between them yawned wider than she'd first thought and she didn't like it. Not one little bit.

'How old are you anyway?'

The smile that had been tugging at the corners of his mouth disappeared. 'Thirty-eight.'

She half-expected him to add 'too old for you', for that was exactly what his sombre expression screamed.

'Mmm…ancient.' She smiled, hoping to lighten the moment.

'I feel it sometimes.' He looked away, as if caught up in some distant memory. 'Not that you'd understand, a carefree woman of the world like you.'

His attitude riled her—she hated being judged, in any way, shape or form.

'I've had my fair share of growing up to do,' she said, placing the document she held on the desk before she crumpled it in her hands. 'Try living with a mother and father who were so staid, so unadventurous, so damn stifling that I had to escape before I burst, only to find that the big, bad world was just that and I had no coping mechanisms to handle it. Call that carefree?'

'I'm sorry; I didn't mean to dredge up old memories. I was referring to your attitude now. I couldn't live the way you do if I tried.'

'Why?' She leaned forward, eager to learn any snippet of information that might give her an insight into her enigmatic boss.

'I'm too entrenched in old-fashioned ideals, too stuck in my ways. No matter what people say, you can't teach an old dog new tricks.' The bitterness in his voice tugged at her heartstrings and she pondered the reason behind it.

'There's nothing wrong with being old-fashioned.' She remembered his kiss, that first tentative touch of his lips as if he'd expected her to rebuff him. It had been nice—heck, it had been fantastic—for a guy to treat her like that rather than just sticking his tongue straight down her throat like the average male did these days. 'It has its advantages, you know.'

'That's not what your report tells me. Nor my staff, for that matter.'

'Well, all the more reason to prove them wrong. Starting with lesson number two, tomorrow.' She tilted her chin up and stared at him, willing him to take the challenge.

He didn't disappoint her. 'Name the time and place and I'm there.'

She stood and headed for the door. 'I'll pick you up again. That way, you don't have an excuse to back out.'

'Are you calling me chicken, Miss Adams?' He smiled and she wished he would do it more often, the simple action illuminating his face and taking ten years off it.

'If the cap fits.' She shrugged and returned his smile, already strategising on the various ways she could get him to smile more than once a day.

'Lady, bring it on.'

She gave him a cheeky wave. 'See you tomorrow, nine sharp. And wear something old.'

'Hey, old is my middle name,' Darcy muttered, watching Fleur sashay out of his office.

As the door closed, he leaned back in his chair and wondered for the hundredth time that week what the hell he was doing fantasising about a woman he couldn't have. As if he hadn't already known about the yawning gap that existed between them, she had to go and reinforce it today by asking about his age, belittling his hobbies and telling him about her parents. What little hope he'd harboured had shrivelled and died about then, as he'd known what she'd implied—he was exactly like them in every way and she despised it.

What he would've given to have had parents like that! Instead, his dad had been an irresponsible drifter, following one harebrained scheme after another and dragging his family around in the process. Darcy had vowed from an early age never to live his life like that so when his parents had died in a freak accident trekking in Nepal, he'd taken control of his life and Sean's, trying to instil different values into his younger brother. Strangely enough, Sean seemed to be the product of genetics rather than environment and had followed in his father's footsteps despite being raised by Darcy from the age of eleven.

As if thoughts of Sean had conjured him up, the intercom on his desk buzzed. 'Your brother to see you, Mr Howard.'

'Thanks, Sheree. Send him in.'

It had been years since Sean had set foot in the office. In fact, if Darcy's memory served him correctly, Sean had sworn he'd never return to the company that had given him a start to his working life when they'd had that rip-roaring argument a few years ago. Sean had wanted to chuck in his job and travel the world, but Darcy had been against it from the start. And, like his parents, Sean hadn't given a damn about what anyone else thought and had followed his dream anyway.

'Hey, bro. Was that Fleur I saw leaving a moment ago? You must be keen, allowing her to visit during office hours and distract you from all this.' Sean sauntered into the office and waved at the mess on the desk. 'By the way, it's nice to see that some things never change.'

Darcy rubbed the bridge of his nose, not in the mood for an argument. Seeing Fleur and hearing what she had to say had left him more drained than he'd realised and all he wanted to do right now was head home, grab some Thai takeaway on the way and settle down to watch his favourite quiz show. 'What's that supposed to mean?'

'The décor. The people.' Sean paused a moment before attempting a sloppy grin. 'You.'

Darcy sat up and shuffled the papers on his desk into some semblance of neatness. 'It's been a long day, Sean. What did you want?'

'Can't a brother just drop in on another?'

'As I recall, you said you'd never set foot inside this place again when you walked out about three years ago. So, whatever you need to say must be damned important for you to ''stoop this low''.'

Sean looked away, obviously recognising the words he'd uttered when he'd resigned from Innovative Imports and told Darcy in no uncertain terms that he would never return. 'I need a favour.'

Darcy's heart sank. He knew that Sean returning home had been too good to be true—Sean must need money, desperately, if he was willing to come here to beg for it.

'What is it this time?' Darcy asked, hoping his disappointment didn't show. He loved his brother and, though he wished things had turned out differently, he would never turn his back on him.

Sean stood up from the chair he'd been slouching in and started pacing the room, as Darcy's unease grew. His brother never paced—he was too cool, too laid-back for that. The favour must be huge.

'I'm going back to uni to finish my business degree and I need to find a company which will employ me on a part-time basis.' Sean cleared his throat before continuing, 'You know, as a kind of job placement.'

Darcy stared at his brother in stunned disbelief, speechless. However, Sean didn't give him much of a chance to respond. 'So, I was wondering if you'd consider employing me again. I know I said some pretty stupid things a few years ago but I'm hoping you'll forgive and forget.'

'No.'

The word hung in the silence between them and he watched Sean deflate before his eyes.

'Thought you might say that,' Sean sighed. 'Look, I'll—'

'No, I won't do you a *favour* by hiring you again.' Darcy tried a frown and failed miserably. 'You'll pull your weight around here like everybody else. Though the boss might be a bit lenient around exam time, with all that extra study you'll have to do.'

Realisation spread over Sean's face. 'You mean it, bro? You'll take a chance on me again?'

Darcy stood up, walked towards Sean and slapped him on the back, almost bursting with pride. 'Yeah, though don't make me regret it.'

'You've got it!' Sean enveloped him in a bear hug while Darcy battled against an uncharacteristic surge of emotion that almost brought tears to his eyes.

'So, does this mean you'll be sticking around?' Darcy disengaged and stepped back, aiming for nonchalance yet knowing Sean wouldn't buy it.

'You betcha! You'll be in your element now, Poppa Bear.'

Darcy smiled, remembering the way Sean used to tease him about his overprotectiveness when he'd been a teenager and thus dubbing him with the nickname. 'Yeah, well, just make sure you don't sit in my chair or sleep in my bed.'

'No problemos. Unless, of course, your bed happens to have the gorgeous Fleur cocooned in there…'

'Get out!'

Sean grinned and opened the door. 'See you at home, bro. And thanks. For everything.'

Sean shut the door before Darcy could respond, leaving him shaking his head and wondering if he'd just woken up from some strange dream. Sean, back at Innovative Imports and here to stay? Who would've predicted that?

'I can't believe I'm paying you money to suck me into these things.' Darcy shook his head and looked around, an expression of bemusement spreading across his face. 'Are these people for *real*?

Fleur grinned and brandished her gun at him. 'Yep. Didn't think you would've tried paintball before, so that's the whole point of bringing you out here. Time to have some more of that fun.'

'Let me get this straight. We drive an hour out of Melbourne to this dump in the middle of nowhere, get changed into camouflage gear, load our weapons with paint bombs and then shoot at every person we see with the hope that I'm the last man standing, so to speak?'

She slow-clapped. 'Give the man a cigar.'

'I must be nuts,' he muttered, hoisting his gun onto his shoulder and staring at the other 'combatants'. 'And by the way, once we get back, you're fired.'

'Spoilsport!' She grinned, admiring the snug fit of his army-green surplus trousers and jacket. For a guy who spent his life behind a desk, his body wasn't half-bad. In fact, it was downright fantastic!

'Stop laughing at me. I look ridiculous enough without you rubbing it in.'

'Oh, poor wittle Darcy,' she said in her best baby voice. 'What are you going to do about it, tough guy?'

'This!'

She should've noticed the gleam in his eye and the change of stance. However, she'd been having too much fun baiting him and therefore her reactions were slower than usual, the first impact sending her sprawling in the dirt.

She lay there, stunned for a moment, before struggling to a sitting position and looking down at the front of her jacket, now covered in fluorescent orange paint.

'Well, well. Will you look at that? Not a bad shot for a novice.' He towered over her, grinning from ear to ear.

'That's it, Rambo. It's war!' While she stood up and dusted off, Darcy ran for the trees after placing his thumb on his nose and wiggling his fingers at her.

Suddenly, the crowd around them erupted into action and everyone followed suit, scattering for cover and yelling like banshees.

Fleur didn't care about dodging other people's paint bombs. She only had one objective in mind—to get Darcy. There was no way she'd let him beat her at this, especially considering it was his first time. Not that she could be considered an expert but she'd be damned if a guy who'd never set foot on a paintball range, let alone played the game before, would oust her.

'I'm really, really scared,' he taunted from behind a tree about ten metres in front of her before sprinting away.

'You asked for it!' she yelled, taking aim and firing at the figure darting between the trees.

'Nice shot!' His laughter echoed in the densely wooded area as he pointed to her paint bomb splattered against a nearby tree trunk. 'Need some practice, huh?'

He stepped from behind a tree and did a little victory dance. 'Ready, aim, fire!'

Fleur's eyes narrowed as she aimed and fired at his gyrating figure, wondering why he'd presented such an easy target yet not particularly caring, as long as she landed at least one shot.

He took the brunt of her paint bomb in the right shoulder, where it exploded and plastered his face in purple.

'Bull's-eye!' She pumped her fist into the air and jumped up and down like an excited child, realising she hadn't had this much fun in ages. So much for teaching Darcy a valuable lesson in how to loosen up—it looked as if she'd learn a few on the way too.

However, her joy seemed premature as she saw him spin around and collapse in a crumpled heap, not moving a muscle.

'Darcy? Are you OK?' She walked towards him with her gun raised, expecting him to leap up and fire at her at any second. However, the closer she got, the more concerned she became. 'Hey, stop kidding around. This isn't funny.'

By the time she reached his side, he still hadn't moved and she knelt beside him, her heart thundering in her chest.

Please let him be all right. She sent a silent plea heavenward as she reached out to touch him, blind panic bringing tears to her eyes and wondering how on earth he could've been hurt by a paint bomb.

'Darcy? Can you hear me?' She leaned over him and stared at his face, expecting to see his eyes spring open any second and for him to yell 'gotcha'.

Instead he lay there, not moving a muscle, sending her hopes plummeting.

Something was terribly wrong and her first-aid training hadn't prepared her for this helpless feeling that reached in and squeezed her heart, rendering her incapable of thinking straight.

'Concentrate,' she mumbled, checking his pulse first before lowering her cheek to his mouth in the hope that he was still breathing. She didn't have a mirror handy to fog up, as the classes had suggested she use to check a person's breathing, so her cheek would have to do.

She sighed in relief as a whisper of warm breath fanned against her cheek—so far, so good. Now all she had to do was turn him into the recovery position and—

'Where am I?' Darcy's eyelids fluttered open and she jumped, all too aware of her proximity to him. His blue eyes focused on her with startling clarity for a person who had supposedly been unconscious and she suddenly knew, without a shadow of a doubt, that he'd been faking it.

However, before she could pull away and deliver a verbal flaying, he wrapped his arms around her and pulled her down on top of him. 'You've checked a few of my vital signs but I think there are a couple you've missed.'

'Let me go!' She squirmed, not willing to acknowledge how right it felt to be cocooned in his arms.

'Starting with this.' He placed her hand over his heart and, to her surprise, it hammered a staccato beat similar to her own.

'And let's not forget this.' He brushed her lips in the lightest of kisses, exerting a gentle pressure designed to entice and leave her begging for more.

'I didn't think you needed mouth-to-mouth,' she murmured as he changed the angle of the kiss, caressing the nape of her neck and pulling her closer.

'Where you're concerned, I need all the TLC I can get.' He deepened the kiss, his tongue easing into her mouth, teasing, taunting, driving her wild with need.

Abandoning all thoughts of stopping, she shifted against him, enjoying the full-length body contact and wishing this were happening somewhere a little more conducive to comfort, somewhere they could fully explore this passion between them that seemed to ignite with the tiniest of sparks.

She should've been the one to break off the kiss, to come to her senses first. In fact, she shouldn't have lost it in the first place!

However, Darcy finally pulled away, a sexy smile playing around his mouth. 'I'm starting to like these lessons you've got planned for me more and more.'

'And I'm starting to like you less and less!' She jumped to her feet and tried to dust herself off, not daring to look at him and risk him seeing what a huge fib she'd just told.

'What did I do?' He hoisted himself off the ground just as quickly and she resisted the urge to shove him back down again.

'Ever heard of the boy who cried wolf? You had me concerned, you great oaf!' She pulled her hair back into its ponytail, assuming it had come undone around the same time as her fleeting resistance to this man.

'I was just having a little fun.' He tried that same sexy smile on her again, the one that had her wishing they were somewhere more private. 'Just like you want me too.'

She grunted in response and turned away, wondering how she'd managed to fall for a guy like Darcy so quickly. He was everything she didn't want in a guy: too staid, too settled, too solid, too *old*. He reminded her of her father, for heaven's sake! And she definitely didn't want a man like that.

So what if he had the looks, the body and kissed like a dream? He wasn't right for her and the sooner she stopped playing with fire, the better.

'By the way, your face is covered in paint. Let me.' He took a handkerchief out of his pocket, reinforcing just how archaic he was—who used hankies these days anyway?—and reached towards her.

'Figures!' she said and stalked away, leaving him grinning.

CHAPTER SIX

DARCY entered the office and walked up to the reception desk rather than bypassing it as he usually did.

'Morning, Sheree. How are you?'

Sheree, who had barely glanced up as he walked in, raised her eyes from the newspaper she'd been reading and stared at him. 'I'm fine, Mr Howard. And you?'

'Couldn't be better.' He smiled at her, a small part of him enjoying her shock. 'Here, try one of these. They're amazing.' He placed a brown paper bag with a muffin in it on her desk before heading towards his own office. 'Oh, and I'm open to all calls today.'

He risked a glance at his receptionist as he closed the door to his office—yes, she was still staring at him in open-mouthed shock, making him more deter-mined than ever to try and incorporate further changes into his business life.

And what about your personal life?

He ignored that thought, not willing to explore it any further at this stage. Fleur had wreaked enough havoc over the last few weeks and he had no intention of taking it to the next level—whatever 'it' was.

As if on cue, a knock sounded at his door.

'Come in.' He cast an eye over his new desk, liking the sleek lines and un-cluttered look. As for the rest of the of-fice, it had turned out even better than expected.

'Darcy, I have the new plans we...' Fleur trailed off as she shut the door and did a full three-sixty-degree turn. 'Wow! When did all this happen?'

'Over the weekend. So, what do you think?' He held his breath, valuing her opinion more than he cared to admit.

'It's fantastic!' She crossed the room, inspecting the prints on the wall, the modern light-fittings, the trendy furniture. 'You've actually moved into the twenty-first century. I'm impressed.'

'All part of the plan.' He shrugged off her compliment as if it meant little while he struggled not to strut around with pride.

She looked at him, her beautiful eyes radiating warmth that left him holding his breath in anticipation. 'It's not easy taking life-changing advice from anyone, yet you've taken it in your stride and actually done something with it. And been a good sport in the process.' She paused, as if struggling to find the right words, and he resisted the urge to pick her up and swing her around with joy. 'You should be proud of yourself.'

He aimed for modest yet knew his grin must've screamed smug satisfaction. 'Thanks.' He gestured around the room. 'This is only the start. Wait till you see what else I've got lined up.'

'I can't wait,' she said quietly, the atmosphere suddenly charged with expectation.

'Speaking of waiting, when do we get to lesson three? It's been a month since I beat you at paintball.' And he'd relived that kiss a thousand times, wishing for a repeat performance; this time, with no clothes between them and Fleur still on top, moaning his name.

'You didn't play fair.' By the blush that crept into her cheeks, she remembered that kiss too and he fully intended to notch up the heat when the opportunity arose again.

'All's fair in love and war.'

Her eyes widened for a moment and he could've sworn she looked ready to bolt. Though he'd been joking, seeing her reaction to the 'L' word disconcerted him. Though she was young, surely she had aspirations to fall in love one day and follow through with the whole ideal—marriage, kids, a mortgage?

'In our case, lucky it was war, huh?' She laughed it off as if the awkward moment had never existed and delved into her briefcase. 'Now, let's get down to business.'

Darcy tried to concentrate on the figures she'd prepared but they swam before his eyes as his attention wandered. His hands itched to reach out and touch her, to tuck a wayward curl behind her ear, to smooth the frown from her brow. He took a steadying breath, which didn't help at all, as a waft of her floral perfume infused his senses and resurrected memories of the other times he'd been close enough to smell it—each time culminating in a kiss that left him hankering for more.

He felt like a teenager who'd barely touched first base and he desperately needed to get to second and third. As for scoring a home run, thoughts of making love to Fleur kept him awake most nights, wishing he could take things faster. But he couldn't; his hands were tied. She'd seen to that, making her feelings about guys who took things too fast more than clear after they'd bumped into Mitch that night.

And though Darcy wanted her more than he'd ever wanted another woman, he wasn't stupid. If Fleur liked taking things slow, he'd do it—hell, he would do anything to ease the tension she'd created by simply walking into his life.

'Are you free this weekend?' The words popped out of his mouth, just as she'd started explaining the latest criteria for assessing profit margins.

'Maybe.' She shuffled the documents in her hands, not quite looking at him.

'There's a new winery I'd like to check out and thought you might be interested in seeing.' It had been far too long since he'd asked a woman out and the fear that she might reject his offer had him sitting on the edge of his seat.

'Sounds good,' she said, sounding more casual than he would've liked.

OK, he hadn't expected her to do cart-wheels or anything but a little more enthusiasm wouldn't have gone astray.

'Though you're not going to try and convert me, are you?' she asked.

'Convert you?'

'Well, I'm trying to help you loosen up. Perhaps you're hoping I'll turn into a wine-tasting, art-loving, tweed-wearing person?'

He tried to ignore the surge of disappointment that followed her cutting words. 'Like me, you mean?'

She had the grace to redden before looking away. 'I haven't seen you wear tweed once.'

'Listen, if you don't want to, that's fine.'

'I'd like to come,' she said and, despite his best intentions to shield his emotions from her, he couldn't deny that the thought of spending a whole day with her away from the office had him excited.

'Fine. Now, where were we?'

So she thought his hobbies were antiquated? He'd show her that just as much fun could be had at wineries as the places she'd taken him. Even more, if he had anything to do with it.

'You've fallen for him, haven't you?'

Fleur glanced up from the depths of her creamy latte and sent Liv a look designed to shut her up. 'I don't want to talk about it.'

'But it's great! About time you had a little romance in your life.'

Fleur frowned. 'I'm not a heroine in one of your novels, you know.'

Liv grinned. 'Obviously not. At least they have more sense than you. When their Mr Right comes along, they grab on to him and don't let go, no matter what the obstacles.'

Fleur cradled her mug and took a sip. 'But what if Mr Right turns out to be Mr Wrong?'

Liv's eyebrows shot up. 'But Darcy's perfect! How could he be wrong for you?'

Fleur had been asking herself that same question for days now. The longer she spent time with him, the more she fell for him despite their obvious differences. Sure, he appeared a little stuffy at times but she liked that about him. She admired his old-fashioned values, his responsible approach to life. She'd dated younger guys who lived each day as if it were their last and she'd been hurt each and every time. Maybe it was time to take a chance on someone different?

'I'm scared, Liv.' There, she'd admitted it. In fact, becoming involved with a steady guy like Darcy terrified her.

'It's because you think he'll play for keeps, isn't it?'

Fleur nodded, her friend's perceptiveness not surprising her. She'd confided in Liv for as long as she could remember and her friend had never steered her wrong, despite her romantic ideals.

'I don't want to end up like my mother, trapped in some dead-end marriage with a man who lives his life strictly to routine.'

'But you love your dad.'

'As a father, yes, but could you imagine being involved long-term with someone like that?' She shuddered, knowing the humdrum existence that accompanied many partnerships, not just her parents' union, would kill her slowly as dreary days drifted into monotonous months, and then into endless years.

Liv leaned forward, her concern evident. 'Is Darcy really like your father?'

Fleur shrugged. 'In all honesty, I can't answer that. I just know that some of his traits are similar and that scares me. Why take a risk with the guy if I know it won't go anywhere?'

'Isn't a fleeting taste of happiness worth it, rather than having nothing at all?' Liv asked.

She drained her coffee and shook her head. 'I wish I knew the answer to that, I really do.'

'Listen to your heart, not your head this time and you'll be fine,' Liv advised.

Fleur managed to smile at her friend, hoping she was right.

Fleur lay back on the picnic rug and closed her eyes, lapping up the sun's rays peeking between the branches of the old gum tree. She could get used to this lifestyle very easily—too easily—if she let go of her reservations and embraced whatever was happening between her and Darcy. She'd pondered Liv's advice to live for the moment and knew her friend had a point, but...

'Hope it's not the company that's putting you to sleep.' Darcy's deep voice drifted over her, the rich tones warming her as much as the dappled sunlight.

'I'm not sleeping, I'm relaxing,' she said, opening her eyes a fraction to peek at him. Lord, he looked good today, clad in khaki shorts and a white polo top that moulded to his muscular torso. She'd never seen him look so casual and she liked it—a lot.

'So I take it the picnic lunch and wine was a hit?'

She rubbed her stomach and groaned. 'No need to fish for compliments. Surely you could tell how much I enjoyed the food by the amount I consumed?'

'Nothing wrong with a healthy appetite.' His tone had turned husky and she suddenly knew he wasn't only talking about the food.

This was it, the perfect opportunity to confront him about his behaviour, particularly those seductive kisses. She should've done it weeks ago but she'd been too frightened, not by his possible reaction but by his potential response. After all, he'd made it more than obvious that he desired her but did she want him in return?

Heck, yes!

'I was just kidding around, you know.' Her eyes flew open at his first tentative touch, his hand reaching out to cup her cheek, and the tenderness she glimpsed in the depths of his eyes almost undid her completely.

She rolled onto her side and propped herself up on an elbow. 'Maybe it's time we stopped kidding around.' There, she'd said it and he hadn't run away, not yet.

He smiled, the simple action lighting up his face, and her pulse responded in typical fashion, galloping at a million beats per minute. 'I thought the whole point of us spending time together was to help me loosen up and now you want me to stop kidding around? Lady, I can't win with you.'

'So you think today's about work?'

His smile slipped a fraction. 'Not exactly.'

'Then what is it about?' She held her breath, almost afraid of his response yet needing to hear it all the same.

'It's about two people spending the day together. Nothing more, nothing less.' He pulled away from her and she missed his brief touch.

She could've dropped the subject there but she'd come too far to back down now. 'Yeah, but you invited me this time. It's not like the other times we've gone out when I've been trying to prove a point to you.'

She knew she'd said the wrong thing as soon as the words left her mouth, for his expression changed from relaxed to downright hostile in a second. 'Tell me this. If I hadn't hired you to turn my company around, would you have gone out with me at all, whether it be at your invitation or mine?'

Her heart plummeted. She owed him the truth if little else. 'Probably not.'

An icy chill settled around her heart at the bleakness in his eyes and she felt compelled to justify her statement. 'We're too different. Our views are opposite in almost every way. It just wouldn't work out.'

'What wouldn't work out?'

'Us.' She didn't know if he was being purposefully obtuse or whether he enjoyed twisting the knife into her heart. For that was what it felt like, as if someone had plunged a huge knife deep inside her and cut off all sense of feeling.

He ran a hand through his hair, the ruffled spikes adding to his air of vulnerability. 'Ever heard the old saying, opposites attract? Or am I just showing my age again?'

'I'm not denying we share an attraction but I get the feeling you want more than that. Would you be happy with just a fling?'

'I'm a man, aren't I?' His laughter sounded bitter and he refused to look her in the eye.

'You're also a stayer, an old-fashioned guy. I, on the other hand, have no aspirations whatsoever to give up my freedom for anybody.' She didn't add 'no matter how great the guy is, or even for someone like you'.

'You think having a relationship means giving up your freedom?'

She nodded, the mind-blowing boredom of her parents' marriage never far from her mind, nor her vow to never, ever become like them. 'I don't think so. I know so.'

'Let me get this straight. You're not interested in having anything more than a fling with me. Is that right?'

He had her there. How could she say yes when she knew that the longer she spent quality time with him, the further she would fall for him? And she had no intention of falling that hard—it just wasn't worth the angst or the pain of picking up the pieces once she moved on.

Yet if she said no, he'd continue giving her the third degree on her motivations behind her behaviour.

'Is that right?' he prompted, fixing her with a probing stare.

'Uh…yeah, I suppose.'

'Try to curb your enthusiasm.' His sarcasm wasn't lost on her and she wished they'd never started this conversation. Or better yet, she wished she'd never taken on his business, no matter how desperate she'd been.

He stood up in one, fluid movement and she couldn't help but admire the way he moved—like the way he walked, with long, confident strides that said 'this man is going places'.

'Fine, have it your way, Fleur.' He held out his hand and helped her up. 'But remember this. Whatever happens, it was your call.'

Fleur switched on the desk lamp, welcoming the flood of light over the fine-print documents spread out in front of her. She hadn't intended on working this late, but when she'd heard Darcy's voice in the corridor outside her office she'd hidden in here till he'd left, determined to avoid running into him. And once she'd stayed she'd decided to get some work done, though it was the last thing she felt like doing on a Thursday evening.

Boy, had she changed! Usually she'd be hitting the town with Liv on a Thursday night, cruising the latest hot spots after eating at a trendy restaurant. However, ever since she'd started this job, she stayed in on week-nights, preferring to curl up and watch a DVD rather than boogying the night away. Pathetic!

Maybe she was becoming more like Darcy? Now, there was a scary thought! Thankfully, he'd steered well clear of her since their winery trip and she couldn't be happier. Though Liv had mentioned she'd lost her spark and Billy had stopped flirting with her at the café, saying she didn't smile much these days.

So what? If it meant protecting her heart and hanging on to her independence, it was worth it.

Rubbing her eyes, she tried refocusing on the figures in front of her.

'Now, what's a spunky girl like you doing locked in here on a Thursday night, huh?'

She looked up and smiled. 'Hey, Sean, I didn't hear you.'

'That's because you've turned into a work freak like my brother.'

'No way!' She beckoned him in. 'Come in and distract me.'

He winked and took a seat opposite her. 'That's the best offer I've had in a long time. How's everything going?'

'Not bad.'

'That good, huh?'

She squared her shoulders, determined not to let him see how flat she felt. 'The work's great. Shouldn't be long till I'm finished up here and Innovative Imports will be a force to be reckoned with again.'

'I wasn't talking about work.' He stared at her, the resemblance to his older brother quite startling.

She fiddled with the hem of her skirt, unwilling to look him in the eyes. 'What else is there?'

'Hey, don't go all shy on me. You know what I'm referring to. You? My brother? This *thing* you seem to have going on?'

Her heart sank. Were her feelings for Darcy that obvious? And if Sean knew, the rest of the office did too. How on earth could she present a professional image when they were probably laughing behind her back?

She looked up, hoping he would buy what she was about to say. 'There's nothing going on. Where did you get that idea?'

He chuckled. 'I mightn't be an Einstein but I can see what's in front of me. My brother, who hasn't been involved with anyone for years, is mooning around like a love-struck dimwit and you practically glow every time he enters a room. So, pardon me for putting the pieces together.'

She shook her head. 'You've got it all wrong.'

'Really?'

Maybe it was the late hour, maybe she was just plain tired, but Fleur suddenly had the urge to confide in Sean.

'OK, maybe we started something. But I don't think it's going anywhere and it's probably better that way. We're too different.'

'Yeah, I can't quite figure why you'd be interested in an old fossil like him.'

'He's not that old.' She jumped to Darcy's defence in an instant and Sean's grin merely widened.

'So what's the problem, then?'

'Darcy wants the whole package and I can't give him that, ever.'

Sean quirked an eyebrow. 'Have you told him that?'

Memories of their discussion at the winery flooded back and she wished things could've been different. She shrugged. 'I'm just not into the whole ''till death us do part'' thing. I need my independence, Darcy needs a commitment. As for anything else...' She drifted off, not wanting to say 'why start something I can't finish?'

'This is heavy stuff,' Sean said, a puzzled look on his face. 'Listen, if there's anything I can do…' He stood, walked around the desk and placed a comforting hand on her shoulder.

'Thanks, Sean.' She leaned her head against his hand, wondering how two great guys like Darcy and Sean could still be single.

'Well, well, well. Now, isn't this a cosy sight. I appreciate my staff putting in overtime but isn't this taking it to extremes?'

Fleur's head jerked upright as Darcy stalked into the office, looking angry enough to fire them both on the spot.

'Settle down, Darcy,' Sean said, casually removing his hand from her shoulder.

However, Darcy acted as if Sean hadn't even spoken. Instead, he fixed her with an icy glare that froze the blood in her veins.

'Please leave, Sean. I need to speak to Fleur. Alone.'

'Don't say I didn't warn you,' Sean muttered as he headed for the door, and Fleur wondered if he spoke to her or Darcy.

However, that seemed the least of her problems as Darcy slammed the door shut and turned to face her.

CHAPTER SEVEN

'DID you want to see me about something?' Fleur asked, her voice a soft, innocent purr that set his blood boiling.

As if his temper hadn't already reached fever-pitch the minute he saw Sean lay a hand on her.

'What was all that about?' He crossed the room in three strides and stood over her desk, hoping her answer wouldn't infuriate him further.

'Sean and I work here. We were having a discussion.' She folded her arms and looked at him, her face an impassive mask that he couldn't read, and it riled him more than he cared to admit.

'He was touching you!' The words sounded ridiculous even to his own ears, but he couldn't take them back once they'd popped out.

To his surprise, Fleur leaped out of her chair and leaned on the desk, her face mere inches from his own. 'You're my boss, not my keeper, and I don't need you coming in here and jumping to conclusions. Just back off, OK?'

Despite the tense atmosphere, he couldn't help but admire her tenacity, her fire. She looked incredible, dark eyes flashing, her lush mouth pursed in disapproval. He'd never been so tempted to lean over and place a kiss on those delectable lips...

As if sensing the shift in his thoughts, she backed away slightly. 'You're unbelievable!'

'No, I'm not. I'm just a man who's crazy. Crazy about you.' He covered the short distance between them in an instant, leaning across the desk and crushing her lips in a kiss intended to prove a point.

This was no soft seduction, no gentle coaxing. And the minute Darcy's lips touched hers, Fleur went up in flames.

She should've struggled, resisted, instead of hanging on to his lapels and dragging him closer, deepening the kiss till they both came up gasping for air.

'Oh, hell,' he muttered, breaking away with a slightly stunned expression on his face.

It was the perfect time to back off, mumble something about hormones and laugh over the situation. However, she didn't do any of those things.

Instead she reached for him and placed her hands against his chest, the radiant heat from his skin scorching her palms through the cotton of his shirt. She splayed her fingers and slowly, torturously, scraped her nails down his torso towards the waistband of his trousers, surprised at her daring yet propelled by some strange force to get closer to him.

'Fleur, this is—'

'Heaven,' she whispered, her soft mouth trailing kisses along his jawline before reaching his lips, where she sucked his bottom lip into her mouth and gently nibbled.

Though she'd never taken lessons in seduction, she thought she was doing a fine job when he let out a groan and half dragged her across the desk, sending papers scattering to the floor.

He pinned her against the desk, his mouth devouring hers as if he was a man starved, a man deprived of the very substance he needed to survive. She answered his hunger, her hands wandering over his body, increasing the heat sizzling between them to unbearable levels.

'I think this is a bad idea,' he groaned as his mouth slid over hers, raining kisses all over her face before dropping lower to her throat.

She'd never been kissed like this and her body melted into a pool of need, a deep-seated yearning that only this man had the power to assuage.

Her head fell back, giving him better access to the sensitive area on her neck. 'Stop thinking, then.'

He nibbled and licked at the exposed skin, notching her excitement up to unbearable levels. His hands reached for the zipper on her dress and, just as he found it and his lips sought hers again, her common sense kicked in.

Despite the urge to throw caution to the wind and finish what they'd started, she broke the kiss.

'This isn't the time or place to be doing this.'

He sighed and leaned his forehead against hers. 'You're right.'

'Why do you always have to be so damn sensible?'

'One of us has to be.' He disengaged from her embrace and stepped away, as if trying to establish some physical distance between them. 'Look, I'm sorry about all this. It won't happen again.'

Now who was sorry?

For some inexplicable reason, tears filled her eyes as she swung away from him and picked up her handbag. She'd wanted him to stop. Hadn't she?

Then why did she have the feeling that she'd just made a huge mistake?

And what was worse, he was acting as if it didn't matter, as if the most passionate encounter she'd ever had with a guy didn't mean a thing.

As she rummaged in her bag for a tissue, he laid a hand on her arm.

'I said I was sorry. Let's just forget the whole thing.'

'You know something? For a smart guy, you can be pretty dumb at times.' And with that parting shot, she dabbed at her eyes and walked out the door without looking back.

Fleur groaned as she hit the play button on her answering machine again.

'Hi, petal. It's your dad here. Just making sure you're coming home for Aunt Ruby's anniversary next weekend. Everyone's looking forward to seeing you. It's been too long, love. See you then. Bye.'

Just when she thought her day couldn't get any worse.

She lay on the couch and closed her eyes, wishing she could think of some plausible excuse to avoid heading home for the party. However, she'd cleverly escaped attending the last three family gatherings in the small country town where most of her family still resided and she didn't think they would tolerate a fourth no-show.

'Great, that's all I need,' she muttered, knowing that her appearance would drag up the usual mind-numbing comments from her parents.

'When are you getting married, love? Have you found yourself a fella yet? Don't leave having kids too late. It's way past time you settled down.' Etc…etc… etc…

She hated every minute of it and would do anything to avoid their nagging. That was one of the main reasons she'd escaped to Melbourne and thrown herself into her studies—anything to get away from the monotonous droning of her boring family.

Whenever the word 'boring' entered her head, she experienced flashbacks of her early conversations with Darcy and how she'd accused him of being just that.

Tonight, he'd certainly proved he was far from boring in the sex stakes. They'd generated enough heat between them to spontaneously combust every last document on her desk and his expertise left her hankering for more. However, true to form, he'd backed away, leaving her body crying out for his soothing touch.

OK, maybe she was being a tad unfair here. She'd been the one to halt proceedings, not him, even though she'd lost her head in the heat of the moment and hadn't cared about what tomorrow might bring. However, that didn't mean good ol' dependable Darcy had had to agree with her.

'Darn it!' She picked up a cushion and started pummelling it, frustrated beyond belief.

If only he could see how infuriatingly sensible he was, then he might actually loosen up enough for them to enjoy each other's company and not think ahead to the consequences.

For that was one conclusion she'd finally reached after weeks of soul-searching; despite chickening out at the last minute and halting proceedings in the office, she had decided to throw caution to the wind and indulge her passion for the man who fuelled her own with a mere glance. She'd been miserable this past week or so, dredging up every reason why they shouldn't get involved— yet what was the point?

She prided herself on her modern outlook on life—why couldn't she instigate an affair and then walk away at the end when it was over? After all, if she went into this with her eyes wide open, surely she couldn't get hurt? And if Darcy would be satisfied with a fling, why shouldn't they go for it?

Suddenly, she sat bolt upright and threw away the cushion as an idea flashed into her mind.

If only Darcy could see how sensible he was...

What better way to prove a point than show the man a potential mirror image of himself in her father—and get her family off her back in the process? Maybe if he saw her parents together first-hand, he might understand where she was coming from in wanting their involvement to be as far removed from that as possible? And maybe, just maybe, they would have a chance after all?

Not to mention the added bonus of having him all to herself for the week-end, in a hotel room, with no space for backing away…

Smiling for the first time that evening, she reached for the phone, looking forward to Aunt Ruby's anniversary party more and more by the minute.

'You didn't tell me you were a country girl.'

'You didn't ask.' Fleur cast surreptitious glances at Darcy as he concentrated on the road. She liked how he drove, with a quiet competence that made her feel safe.

'I bet there's a lot I don't know about you.'

'Don't worry, my family will fill you in.' She inwardly groaned, knowing that the weekend would be torture for her yet glad for the opportunity to further her plans for Darcy.

He chuckled. 'I can't wait. Though it sounds like you're not too keen.'

'I've already warned you. They're going to jump to all sorts of conclusions about us, not to mention embarrass me.' If her father's curiosity on the phone had been anything to go by, Darcy was in for a harder time than he thought.

'Don't worry about me. I can handle them. Can you?'

'Just don't encourage them, OK?'

'Would I do something like that?' Though he kept his gaze focused on the road, he wore a grin that stretched from ear to ear and her heart thudded in response.

'Hell, yes!' She laughed, enjoying the easygoing camaraderie that had sprung up between them over the last week.

She'd assumed things would be awkward following the interlude in her office yet surprisingly he'd been just as happy as her to avoid the issue. And when she'd invited him to accompany her to the family gathering, he'd been more than willing to oblige. Maybe he thought they could pick up where they'd left off in her office?

She'd sure hoped so and Liv had egged her on, saying the weekend away was the perfect opportunity to seduce him. And after much debating over endless coffees and muffins at the café, she'd given in and agreed. She would pull out all stops over the weekend away with Darcy and see where a little romance in her life would take her.

In fact, she had it all planned out: book a motel room, turn off her voice of reason and let him turn her on with some of that kissing he was so good at.

However, her master plan to throw caution to the wind and enjoy her time with Darcy had been thwarted in true Edwardian fashion. Despite her booking into a nearby motel for the weekend, her parents wouldn't hear of it and had insisted she and Darcy stay with them— which meant separate bedrooms, of course.

She'd cancelled the motel reservation with reluctance, her dreams of showing Darcy how liberated she could be—starting with *one* room and a king-sized bed—vanishing. Instead she'd have to be satisfied with proving her point to him by introducing him to her parents and their archaic ideals, in the hope that he'd do the opposite and run straight into her welcoming arms for whatever time period they had left once they returned to Melbourne.

'Is that the turn-off?' He pointed to a roadside mailbox and chuckled. 'The Adams family, huh?'

She shook her head, a host of memories flooding back. 'I can't believe they haven't changed that sign yet. I used to get teased at school all the time, about our family being monsters and freaks.'

'Well, I've seen you at your worst and let me tell you, it ain't pretty!'

She punched him playfully on the arm. 'I've got nothing on my mother. Wait till you see her first thing in the morning, with her hair in curlers, wearing her pink chenille robe. Ugh!'

'Do women still do that hair-in-curlers stuff?'

'You tell me. It's around your vintage, isn't it?'

Rather than berating her, which he would've done several weeks ago, he joined in her laughter. 'There's nothing wrong with the right vintage. I'm like a fine wine, getting better with age.'

'Yeah, but if you're cellared for too long, you'll go off.'

As he steered the car under the shade of a towering eucalypt and switched off the engine, he turned towards her and reached out to caress her cheek. 'Oh, I'm about to go off all right.'

Her eyes widened at his innuendo, her pulse racing in anticipation. 'Promises,

promises,' she said, turning her head slightly and bringing his thumb in contact with her lips.

As if sensing her invitation, he stroked her bottom lip repeatedly while cupping her chin. 'Us old fellas know how to keep a promise. Didn't you know that?'

'I'm counting on it.' She opened her mouth, letting her tongue flick out to capture his thumb, watching his pupils dilate with passion. She'd never been this brazen before, though by the look on his face she knew she was doing something right.

He moaned and closed his eyes momentarily as his head lolled back on the headrest. 'Do you have any idea what you do to me?'

'You'll just have to tell me,' she said, nibbling a moment longer before dropping his hand quickly.

Though she would've liked to continue, she'd just caught sight of her parents, who were practically falling over themselves in their haste to make it to the car.

'What the—?'

'It's showtime,' she said, pointing to the incoming assault and grimacing.

Darcy had class, she'd give him that much. Though Fleur loved her parents, she couldn't stand being in their overbearing presence for more than half an hour at a time, yet here Darcy was, listening to her father's droning commentary on the local football side and her mother's endless prattle about the Country Women's Association. Not to mention fielding several probing questions regarding his 'intentions'. She'd managed to deflect most of the heat away from him. Until now.

'Petal, once you and Darcy have finished your tea, perhaps you'd like to rest and freshen up before the party?' Her dad had called her petal for as long as she could remember; he thought it was amusing, a play on words for Fleur. She found it anything but.

'Good idea, Dad.' She practically leaped to her feet, eager to escape to the sanctity of her room.

'Now, about rooms…' Her dad shuffled his feet uncomfortably, as if reluctant to broach the subject.

Once again, Darcy came to the rescue. 'I don't want to impose, Mr Adams. I'm more than happy to take a room at the local motel.'

Her father sagged in relief. 'That's great, Darcy. It's just that we're a bit crowded here, what with the family and all—'

'If you don't mind, could you take Fleur with you?' her mum interrupted and they all turned to stare. 'I mean, the house isn't terribly large and I'm afraid I've overbooked the family. Do you mind, dear? Darcy?'

Fleur tried not to gape as she took in her mother's flushed cheeks, her bright eyes. If she didn't know any better, she'd swear that her mum was trying to give them some privacy. Impossible, as her mum's rules about boys in the house, let alone bedrooms, had been as strict as her father's when she'd been growing up.

'Florence!' Her dad's scandalised tone galvanised Fleur into action.

'No problem, Mum. Darcy and I will stay at the motel in town.' She hugged her mum, the first genuine expression of love she'd shown her in a long time. 'See you at the party, Dad.' She pecked her dad on the cheek and stared at Darcy over his shoulder, making eyes towards the door and hoping he'd get the drift.

Thankfully, he did. 'It's been a pleasure meeting you both. I'll see you at the party.' He shook hands with her dad, who still looked on the verge of having an apoplectic fit, and kissed her mother on the cheek, her blush deepening.

Fleur hid her elation till they reached the safety of the car, where she let out a joyous whoop.

Darcy turned to her, a speculative gleam in his eyes. 'Looks like it's just you and me, kid.'

CHAPTER EIGHT

FLEUR held her breath as she strode to the front desk of the Springwood Motel, looking as if she made reservations every day of the week. When in fact her knees fairly shook at the prospect of spending the night with a man who had turned her well-ordered world upside down since the moment she'd first met him.

Ever since she'd invited him on this weekend away, her mind had shifted into overdrive—was she doing the right thing? Would he read more into it than she wanted? And the biggie of them all: what if she fell for him—deeper than she already had, that was. For despite her vows to maintain her independence and never become involved in a heavy relationship that could end up in a marriage like her parents', she knew that Darcy had the power to undermine her resolve. And it scared her. It scared her to death.

She'd thought he might be shocked by her invitation for a weekend away yet he'd hidden his surprise well, obviously not willing to push her for the reason behind her turnaround. Was he thinking that she shoved him away one minute, and then invited him away for a dirty weekend the next? The man must be confused as hell though, if he had any sense, he probably assumed that since when did the machinations of the female mind have any logic to them? Thankfully, he'd accepted her invitation and, though she'd tried to play it cool, she'd been in a frenzy of anticipation ever since.

She'd warned him about her parents' old-fashioned views, especially when it came to sleeping arrangements, and, to her chagrin, he hadn't seemed to mind. So much for the 'dirty' part of the weekend!

And now this. In some weird twist of fate, her mum had finally entered the twenty-first century and almost rushed them out the door and into the local motel. Though Fleur couldn't figure out her mum's motivation behind the biggest turnaround in history, she'd made the trip from her parents' home to the motel in record time—just in case her folks changed their minds and her dad came after Darcy with a shotgun.

She tried to act nonchalant when the proprietor finally appeared, while her insides churned in a mixture of nerves and anticipation. 'I had a booking which was cancelled earlier this week. I was wondering if the room was still available?'

'Fleur Adams? You're Flo and Maurie's little girl, aren't you?'

'That's right. Is the room still available?'

The owner nodded. 'Sure is. Would you like me to show you up to the room?'

'That would be great.' She turned towards Darcy, the edgy look on his face surprising her. What did *he* have to be nervous about? She was about to make his day. 'Is that OK with you?'

'Sounds good to me.' Darcy tried to instil a certain degree of calm into his voice, when all he felt like doing was sweeping her into his arms and carrying her up the staircase to their room.

Their room. The mere thought of it had him more excited than he'd been in a long time. What was it about this woman that had him so eager he could barely restrain himself?

Sure, she was beautiful, but it was so much more than that: her lively personality, her ability to laugh at herself and, dared he admit it, her instinct to let her hair down and have fun, all combined to make her one special lady. And he had every intention of showing her what she meant to him this weekend.

He followed her up the stairs and into the first room on the left, trying to ignore the curious stares of the proprietor, who kept glaring at him as if he was about to ruin the town virgin's reputation. He probably should be feeling a tad guilty; after all, news would spread like wildfire that the prodigal daughter had returned to Springwood with an older suitor in tow—and had shared a room with him!

However, guilt was the furthest emotion from his mind when Fleur slammed the door shut on the nosy owner and turned towards him. 'Well, that's it, then.'

'Did I miss something?' He placed their overnight bags on the floor and headed for the window, seeing the rolling hills and green pastures but not really absorbing their beauty. His nerves were stretched taut and he had a feeling that it wouldn't take much to get them to snap.

'Your reputation in this town will be ruined.' She managed to keep a straight face, though the corners of her mouth twitched with the effort.

'It's not mine I'm worried about.' He smiled, though searched her face for any indication that she felt uncomfortable with their arrangement.

'Hey, don't give it a second thought. I wouldn't have booked one room if I gave a damn what people here thought about me.'

'What about your family?'

She folded her arms, the half-smile vanishing. 'I'm not under their roof any more so I can do what I please.'

He walked towards her and laid a comforting hand on her shoulder. 'Why the rebel act?'

'It's not an act.' She shrugged off his hand, picked up her bag and pretended to fiddle with the zip.

By her tense body language, he knew he had to tread carefully beyond this point. 'I hardly know your folks but it's pretty obvious they love you. Why are you so defensive about them?'

'I'm the psychologist here, not you,' she snapped, unzipping her bag with particular force. 'Besides, you wouldn't understand.' He only just caught her muttered, 'You're just like them.'

Her throwaway comment irked him more than it should have. Did she still see him as boring, stodgy, stuck in his ways? And if so, why invite him up here to spend the weekend with her?

Shaking his head, he headed to the door. 'I'm going for a stroll around the town.'

She managed a terse, 'Fine,' before ignoring him again.

'Do we leave for the party at seven?'

She nodded and avoided his eye. 'If you don't mind, I'll see you down at the hall. I promised mum I'd arrive early to help with the food.'

'OK. See you there.' He shut the door quietly, when he actually felt like slamming it shut.

So much for romance this weekend.

* * *

Fleur knew she'd overreacted to Darcy's questioning this afternoon but she couldn't help it. To be back in this town was bad enough; to have her reasons behind her behaviour analysed was too much. Besides, she'd been edgy enough when they'd arrived at the motel, wondering what she'd say or how she'd act once they reached the confines of their room. Planning a seduction was one thing, but putting the plan into action another.

She'd aimed for cool and had come out sounding like a petulant child, sending him packing in the process. And now they'd had to spend the evening together, fielding all sorts of probing questions and veiled hints about their relationship 'status' which he'd handled with aplomb yet left her gritting her teeth. Bunch of nosy old busybodies! And that was just her extended family.

As for the speeches…when Aunt Ruby had stood up on the stage, hand in hand with Uncle Jack, and reiterated her love of fifty years, she'd stared pointedly at Fleur and mumbled something about there being no greater gift and that young people of today needed to get their priorities right. Almost every head in the hall had turned to stare at her and she'd wished the floor would open up and swallow her. Thankfully, Darcy had squeezed her hand and she'd smiled her gratitude, wondering what she'd done to deserve a guy like him.

'Let's get out of here,' she said, hoping her eyes conveyed a clear message and wondering what he would do about it after her earlier treatment of him.

'The party does seem to be winding down.'

She smiled and arched an eyebrow. 'On the contrary, the party is just getting started.'

His eyes widened in surprise before darkening to midnight-blue as he placed his hand in the small of her back and gave her a gentle nudge towards the door. 'After you.'

Fleur's pulse tripped in excitement as they said their goodbyes and strolled back to the motel, hand in hand.

'Thanks for being here tonight.' She'd resorted to small talk again, which didn't inspire her with confidence.

'Thanks for inviting me.' His polite response didn't help. In fact, it left her floundering for the next thing to say.

She looked up at the stars, feeling like the Fleur Adams of old: shy, naïve, wishing a boy would like her. In fact, strolling with Darcy along the main street of Springwood reminded Fleur of her debutante night, when Nick Davey had held her hand and tried to kiss her at the end of the evening, leaving her bewildered and out of her depth. Strangely enough, being in Darcy's presence made her feel like that all the time, which was one of the reasons she was so determined to go through with this tonight.

'It's a beautiful night,' he said, pausing at the entrance to the motel. 'But not as beautiful as you.'

He stared at her with barely concealed passion and her stomach somersaulted before dropping away in nervous anticipation.

'Thanks. Shall we go up?' She aimed for nonchalance, as if she invited men up to her room every night of the week.

He nodded and clasped her hand tighter, drawing her towards him and looping an arm around her shoulders. They traversed the stairs in silence as the butterflies fluttering in Fleur's stomach took flight.

'Are you sure about this?' He unlocked the door and ushered her into the room.

She'd never been so unsure of anything in her life but being with Darcy felt right, as if it was the most natural thing in the world. She wanted to be happy—*deserved* to be happy—and maybe it was time to take a risk and see what happened?

She wrapped her arms around his neck and gazed into his eyes. 'Drop the chivalry, Darcy. At least for tonight.'

A hint of a smile played around his mouth, wicked with promise, and her eyes drifted shut as she anticipated the first scintillating contact of his lips on hers. However, he surprised her by stroking a fingertip across her forehead, slowly down her nose, skimming her mouth and trailing down her jaw and collarbone to rest at the point where her cleavage started.

Her breath hitched as he toyed with the button there, her limbs growing heavy as desire snaked through her body.

'I've been wanting to do this all night,' he murmured, undoing the buttons of her blouse with infinite patience while his lips worked a slow, burning trail from her earlobe to her mouth.

She sighed as his hands finally came into contact with her bare skin at the same time his mouth closed over hers, sending her senses spiralling. She ached to feel him, to taste him, to savour this night together.

As if sensing her need, he deepened the kiss while his hands unhooked her bra in one, deft movement, leaving her burning for his touch. She shivered as he cupped the weight of her breasts, his thumbs moving in slow, concentric circles, fuelling her need to feel his body pressed against hers. She arched against him, as if she couldn't get enough—and they'd barely started!

He broke the kiss to stare at her, desire mixed with amusement visible in his eyes. 'If you want to have your way with me, go ahead. I won't stop you.'

'Thanks for the vote of approval.' She slid his shirt off, admiring his toned torso, eager to explore the ridges of hard muscle with her hands, her mouth.

She rained tiny kisses across his chest, her hands skimming the broad, muscular expanse.

He groaned and reached for her, pulling her flush until her breasts flattened against his chest, the light smattering of hair rasping across her nipples and taking her pleasure to new heights.

'You're driving me crazy.' He backed her towards the bed, maintaining body contact the whole way.

'Lucky for you, I'm a psychologist,' she murmured, her hands exploring the contours of his back while she nuzzled his neck. 'And I have every intention of giving you a very private, one-on-one consultation...'

CHAPTER NINE

As if Darcy hadn't already guessed, he now knew for sure. He'd fallen for Fleur in a big way and last night had sealed it. They'd made love repeatedly, her insatiable appetite driving him wild—and almost leaving him feeling his age this morning. So much for his intentions to take things slow; the minute they'd reached their room, he hadn't been able to keep his hands off her, not that she seemed to mind.

He'd never met a woman so in tune with her own body and her needs—and it scared him. A lot. Though she hadn't given him time to think about it last night, he'd been plagued by self-doubt this morning, wondering what a woman like her could see in a guy like him. And her behaviour since hadn't reassured him.

While he'd been prepared to discuss what had happened between them and explore where they went from here, she seemed quite content to act as if having mind-blowing sex all night wasn't an unusual occurrence.

Perhaps it wasn't for her?

He shook his head, dismissing the thought in an instant. She didn't seem like that sort of girl, though what did he really know about her? Apart from the fact she liked to live life to the fullest and had limited tolerance for those who didn't, did he *really* know her?

No matter. He would find out what made her tick. After all, he needed to know more about the woman he intended to marry.

'Here we are.' She stopped the car outside his house, leaving the engine running.

'Why don't you come in for a while?' *Like forever.*

'No, thanks. I've got things to do.' She barely looked at him, preferring to glance over his left shoulder.

'But it's Sunday,' he persisted, not willing to let her go that easily. He wanted to take her inside and show her that last night hadn't been a one-off, that they could repeat the magic time and time again. He wanted to lose himself in her, to hold her in his arms on his turf and never let go. He'd never been a player and the feelings she aroused in him made it more than clear that he wanted to play for keeps with this woman.

'Look, Darcy, the weekend was fun. But it's time to get back to the real world now.' Her short, clipped tone surprised him. Though they hadn't spoken much on the drive back to Melbourne, at least she'd been civil.

Suddenly, a horrifying thought insinuated its way into his mind. 'Don't tell me last night was about you trying to teach me another lesson?'

A slight frown marred her brow. 'I don't understand.'

'You just said the weekend was fun. Was that what last night was too? Just another lesson in how to get stuffy old Darcy to have fun?'

She shook her head but wouldn't meet his eyes. 'It wasn't like that.'

'Then why the attitude? Why give me the brush-off? And what's all this about the real world?' He fired the questions at her, needing to hear her answers yet knowing he wouldn't like them.

She finally looked at him and the bleakness in her eyes cut him to the core. 'The real world is where we both live, two very different people who coexist for a short space of time before moving on. Life isn't a fantasy, like last night was.'

The words 'moving on' penetrated the fog pervading his brain and he rebelled against them with every fibre of his being. 'Why do we have to move on? Don't you believe in happy-ever-after?'

Her mouth dropped open. 'You're talking long-term commitment?'

'Hell, yes!' His voice had risen several octaves and he controlled it with difficulty. 'Why not?'

To his amazement, she laughed, a bitter sound that sent his hopes plummeting. 'Let me get this straight. We spend a weekend away together and you want to jump into a full-on relationship? God, you really do belong on the ark!'

He stared at her in disbelief, wondering how he could've misread her signals and feeling like an absolute fool in the process.

'I'm sorry, Darcy. It's just that—'

'See you at the office.' He stepped from the car, slammed the door and walked up the front path without looking back.

It had been one hell of a week and, once again, Fleur was buried to her neck in paperwork when she should've been hitting the town with Liv. Though working late did have its advantages; she'd successfully avoided Liv's phone calls for most of the week, knowing that her friend would expect a blow-by-blow description of her weekend away with Darcy. And right now she could barely think about it, let alone talk about it.

What an unmitigated disaster! She'd known Darcy was old-fashioned but hey, expecting a long-term commitment after one night together? The mind boggled.

OK, maybe she'd been overly harsh in labelling the most incredible experience they'd shared as a 'weekend away'. However, it had been the only way she could get Darcy to back down from his ridiculous idea that they belonged together. And from what he'd been saying, she wouldn't have been surprised if he'd popped the question right then and there.

Despite the wonderful way they'd connected—in and out of the bedroom—she had no intention of ever heading down the matrimonial path with any man, even one as special as Darcy, and spending the weekend back in Springwood and seeing her parents merely reinforced the fact.

Her plan had backfired—rather than Darcy seeing the resemblance between him and her parents, she'd let her guard down and realised something she'd been trying to ignore for a while. She'd fallen for a man totally wrong for her and making love with him had cemented her feelings.

In one way, she'd been flattered by his wish to enter into a committed relationship, meaning he probably reciprocated her feelings. However, she didn't want the responsibility of breaking his heart when she moved on—as she would at some time in the future. Staying in one place, one job, one city wasn't enough for her. She needed to prove her independence and a steady guy like Darcy

wouldn't go for that sort of lifestyle, ever.

So what had she done about it?
Thrown herself into the job at hand,
which was quickly drawing to a close.
The change in staff attitudes at
Innovative Imports had been astounding
and, as a result, productivity and profit
margins were rising every day. She'd
done what she'd set out to do and that
was change the company's and the
CEO's way of thinking. Her job satisfaction should've been at a premium, especially considering this was her first real
project. Then why did she feel a strange
sadness mingled with relief that her ten-
ure here was coming to an end?

She closed her eyes and rubbed her
temples, knowing it was time to call it a
night yet reluctant to head home to her
empty apartment. At least she didn't have

time to think at work; once she arrived home, her thoughts took flight, making rest or sleep impossible. In fact, she'd hardly managed three hours a night since last weekend and knew it showed. Little wonder Darcy had been avoiding her—she looked a fright!

'OK, enough's enough! Why are you holding out on me?'

Fleur's eyes flew open at the sound of Liv's voice. 'What are you doing here?' She tried to instil some enthusiasm into her voice yet came up wanting.

'Girl, you look awful! What's happened?' Typical Liv, straight to the point, though her accurate observation didn't help Fleur's state of mind.

Fleur waved at the neatly ordered papers on her desk. 'It's hard being an exec but someone's got to do it.' If she aimed for levity, perhaps Liv would leave her alone. Predictably, she didn't.

'Let's see. You've avoided all my phone calls, didn't return my messages and haven't been near the gym or café all week. Something on your mind, sweetie?'

To Fleur's annoyance, tears sprang to her eyes. 'You could say that.'

'Hey, things must be bad for you to turn on the waterworks.' Liv delved in her handbag and held out a tissue. 'What gives?'

'Darcy wants us to be a couple.' The words popped out of her mouth in a second and she instantly regretted it.

'He what?' Liv screeched, flopping into the nearest chair.

'Stupid, huh?' Fleur dabbed at her eyes, wishing she didn't like the sound of those two words—Darcy and couple—together so much.

'No way.' Liv clapped her hands together, her eyes sparkling with excitement. 'This is so cool. Imagine, meeting at the café like that and ending up together. It's so romantic!'

'Yeah, just like one of your corny novels, huh?'

'Hey, they're not so corny now. Look at you. Your life could be a novel!'

Fleur shook her head. 'It is, though my story doesn't have the happy ending.'

Liv's eyes narrowed. 'You knocked him back, didn't you?'

'Of course!' Fleur snapped, wishing she'd never opened her big mouth. 'I can't stay with him.'

'Why not?'

Fleur wished she could give Liv a thousand reasons, starting with 'I don't love him', 'he's not my type of guy' or 'I can't imagine spending the rest of my life with him'. However, she couldn't say any of those things because they weren't true so she settled for the reasons that she'd been reciting to herself all week.

'He's too old for me, we have little in common and he reminds me of my dad.' The excuses sounded lame, even to her own ears.

'There's no pleasing you, is there? And I can't believe you're still hung up over your parents.'

Fleur sighed. 'It's not a hang-up, I just don't want to end up like them.'

'Happy?' Liv spoke quietly and Fleur knew her friend meant business. 'Not everyone's cut out for the high life, you know. Why can't you just accept that they love their life and you move on with yours?'

'Because I'm scared that, no matter what I do or how far I run, I'll still end up like them. Dull, boring stick-in-the-muds.' There, she'd voiced her number-one fear and hadn't been struck down by lightning.

'And you reckon Darcy comes from the same mould?'

Liv's raised eyebrows clearly demonstrated her incredulity.

Fleur nodded, too upset to speak.

Liv stared at her before jumping out of the chair and grabbing her handbag. 'Come on. Time to get you absolutely smashed.'

'I'm not in the mood, Liv.'

Liv almost hauled Fleur out of her seat. 'Well, I am. Let's go.'

Feeling more dejected by the minute, Fleur had no option but to follow.

*   *   *

Darcy waited until the girls had left before locking up and heading home. He'd been about to oust them from the office when he'd overheard part of their conversation, which had stopped him dead. So that was why Fleur had taken him home to meet her folks—she thought he was just like them: *dull, boring stick-in-the-muds*. Her words echoed through his head till he felt like screaming.

So much for his killer charm! She'd probably slept with him out of some warped sense of pity than anything else. How could he have been so wrong? He'd thought they shared something special, starting with that first kiss at the night-club, and he'd been willing to explore it, not expecting to fall in love along the way. To stupidly, foolishly, fall in love with a woman who thought he was long past it. She'd said it so many times, in so many different ways, yet he hadn't wanted to believe it.

He might be old but he sure wasn't wise!

Letting himself into the house, he headed for the lounge. Though he wasn't a drinker, he needed a shot of brandy to warm the chill that had settled deep in his gut since he'd heard Fleur's words.

'It's not like you to hit the bottle.' Sean wandered into the room and Darcy glared at him, taking a swig from the balloon glass in his hand. 'What's up?'

'Haven't you got something better to do with your time than harass me? Like homework?'

Sean sank onto the couch and stretched out. 'Nah, this is much more fun.'

'Go away.' Darcy cradled the balloon in his hand and stared into the swirling amber liquid, wishing he could get blotto, wake up and forget about the whole damn mess.

'Lovers' tiff? Makes sense, seeing as Fleur's expression around the office these days matches yours.'

'I don't want to talk about it.' Darcy took another sip of brandy before he did something totally out of character, like fling the remainder of his drink in Sean's face.

'Well, you need to talk about it. Come on, man. Get it off your chest.'

To his surprise, Darcy found that the thought of confiding in Sean mightn't be such a bad idea. 'She thinks I'm dull, boring and too old. Hell, she thinks I'm like her father!'

'Prove her wrong.' Sean spoke so quietly that Darcy thought he'd misheard.

'What?'

'You heard me. If you love this woman and I think you do, prove to her that she's wrong about you. Win her over.'

Darcy stared at Sean as if he'd just spoken a language he didn't understand.

Sean continued, 'It's not that hard. Show her the side of you she wants to see. Take her completely by surprise. Sweep the lady off her feet. What have you got to lose?'

Everything.

Darcy wouldn't dare voice his thought for fear it might come true.

CHAPTER TEN

FLEUR hated gardening so she knew she must be feeling even worse than she originally thought when she donned gloves, picked up the few tools she owned and headed for the front courtyard of her apartment. She'd deliberately avoided renting a house for that very reason, yet the apartment she'd lived in for the last few months boasted a small lawn and flowerbeds that required occasional attention, much to her disgust.

She sat in the sunshine, enjoying the unseasonal burst of hot weather yet knowing Melbourne's fickle climate might provide rain and hail by the end of the spring day. Stabbing at the weeds that dared poke their heads through the soil proved to be more therapeutic than antic-ipated and she'd soon cleared away most of them. Pruning had been next on her agenda, though the roar of a motorcycle gunning up her street distracted her.

'Hoons,' she muttered, accidentally snipping off a rosebud.

Rather than the noise abating, it inten-sified, and she craned her neck to see who was making the racket. Surprisingly, the bike skidded to a halt in front of her gate and she leapt up, shading her eyes to see who the visitor was. Now that the noise had died down to a dull roar, she could admire the machine, a gleaming new Harley.

As for the rider...leather encased long legs, muscular thighs and broad shoul-ders, the tinted visor adding an air of mystery to the man. He must be lost, for she didn't know anyone who owned a bike, though Mitch had constantly whined about his lack of funds to do so.

By the build of this guy, he definitely wasn't Mitch.

She strolled towards the figure encased in top-to-toe black leather, wishing she could see behind the visor. As if answering her prayers, the rider slowly took off the helmet, inch by inch, as if keeping her in suspense.

'Fancy a ride?' Darcy grinned like a little boy who'd just received the best Christmas present ever and Fleur stopped dead, unable to assimilate the shadowy figure on a killer set of wheels with the man she'd labelled as dull.

'What are you doing on that thing?' she finally managed to spit out, trying her best not to gawk.

He caressed the shining chrome and in a blinding flash, Fleur wished she were under him and taking some of that same treatment. 'I've always wanted a Harley and I figured now was as good a time as any. Do you like it?'

She nodded, unprepared for the swift rush of excitement that surged through her body as she openly admired the man perched on his new toy.

'So, are you coming for that ride or not?' His cocky smile increased the heat between them, leaving her breathless.

She should be over this by now. She'd done her best over the last week, schooling her reactions towards the man, aiming for pleasant and professional. Yet in half a minute he'd torn down her carefully erected barriers, leaving her feeling like an inexperienced teenager all over again.

'I'd like that.' Sounding painfully shy, she shucked off her gloves, tossed them over the fence and climbed on the back of the Harley as he handed her a helmet.

'Hold on tight,' he said as he revved the engine and took off from the kerb, leaving her with no option but to do exactly that.

She wrapped her arms around his waist, the vibrations of the bike combined with the sensation of being pressed against his body doing weird and wonderful things to her insides. She'd never been on the back of a motorbike before and found the experience more exhilarating than she'd imagined. Or was that the man taking her for a ride?

After an all-too-brief stint around the block, he pulled up outside her apartment, leaving the engine running.

She clambered off the back, her body infused with a strange reluctance to relinquish her hold on him.

'Thanks, that was great.' She handed him back the helmet and ran a hand through her curls, knowing she must look a fright. However, the way Darcy stared at her, she suddenly didn't care.

'Any time.' He gave her a quick salute before pushing his visor down and riding away, leaving her staring after him in confusion.

What just happened here? She had no idea.

Darcy rode to work the next morning, shocking everyone in the office when he strolled in wearing his leathers. Rather than laughing at him, which he'd half expected, his staff had crowded around, firing questions at him and showing their genuine interest. And when he'd pulled out his latest party trick, the strange yo-yo like device called a diabolo that he'd ordered over the internet, his staff had joined in the fun and begged to have a turn.

He sensed rather than saw Fleur enter the office, wondering what she thought of all the frivolity. She'd been right in her appraisal of his staff and, now that he'd taken her advice on board, the turnaround at the company had been nothing short of amazing. Though his change in attitude had been what was needed, he gave credit where it was due and in this case it lay solely at the feet of the woman who'd turned both his business and his life around.

'OK, folks, back to work.' He smiled as good-natured groans filled the air and he headed to his office, where he changed out of his leathers and into the spare suit he kept hanging in a cupboard.

A knock on the door sounded as he finished knotting his tie. 'Come in,' he called out, wrenched out of his little fantasy of Fleur entering his office while he was undressed.

The woman in question entered the room and he bit back a smile. 'Hi, how are you?'

'Fine, thanks.' Though little could mar her beauty, he thought her words didn't match her appearance these days. She looked worn out and he wondered if she'd had a hard time sleeping, like him. 'What was all that laughter about out there?'

'Oh, nothing much. I just showed some of the girls my diabolo.'

'Pardon?' Her eyebrows shot up as the cheeky grin he'd grown to love spread across her face.

'Care to take a look?' He kept a straight face while reaching under the desk.

Her grin widened. 'Are you sure I haven't seen it already?'

'Tsk, tsk.' He produced the device and held it out to her. 'There. Are you impressed?'

'What is that?' She stared at it and he wished they could've continued their word games a tad longer. They hadn't teased each other like this in ages and he'd missed it.

'It's a cross between a yo-yo and juggling. Apparently, it originated in China two thousand years ago and is good for people stuck in an office all day. You just head out to the local park and try diabolo-ing for twenty minutes a day.'

'Are you feeling all right?' The twinkle in her eyes set his heart pounding and he wished they could start over, without all the misunderstandings and judgement calls.

'Never better. Life's too short not to try new things, don't you think?'

She nodded, though he could tell he hadn't convinced her just yet. 'Speaking of new things, here's the latest run-down of the company's figures. I think you'll be pleased.' She paused for a moment, before handing the documents over. 'It also means that my work here is done. I'll probably finish up by the end of the week, if that's all right with you?'

He took the documents she'd prepared, wanting to say that no, it wasn't all right, not by a long shot. He needed her in his life and he'd be damned if he just sat back and let her walk out of it. However, he needed to stick to his plan if he had any chance of making this work.

'Fine.' He didn't look up from the papers he studied. 'Why don't you let me take you out to dinner, as a thank-you for all you've done?'

She didn't answer immediately and he was forced to look up at her. A multitude of emotions flickered across her face before she finally spoke. 'That sounds nice. Where and when?'

He resisted the urge to pump his fist into the air. 'Why don't you leave the details to me? Oh, and good work, Fleur. You've done a great job.' He returned to studying the papers, knowing she'd take it as a dismissal.

'Thanks.'

She walked out of his office, leaving Darcy with a smug grin and myriad ideas whirling through his head.

'Help me out, Sean. I have no idea where to take her to dinner. It needs to be somewhere different, out of the ordinary.' Darcy had barged into Sean's room after a single knock on the door, eager for his brother's advice. He hadn't steered him wrong so far and, God forbid, he was actually counting on his help now.

'Chill out, man. Let me think.' Sean lay back on his bed, hands behind his head. 'So the rest of the plan is working?'

Darcy shrugged, flooded by a sudden rush of insecurity. Though he was a grown man, Fleur made him feel like a schoolboy most of the time, one who didn't know the right things to say or do. 'The Harley impressed her. Not sure about the diabolo.'

'She obviously likes speed and machines…' Sean sat up and clicked his fingers. 'I've got it! How about a mystery flight?'

The idea took root in Darcy's mind and grew. 'Yeah, not bad, little brother. What better way to show her that I'm a spur-of-the-moment kinda guy then book a flight to goodness knows where? She'd love that. We could end up in Cairns, Darwin, maybe Perth?' Each and every one of those destinations held appeal, because he'd get to spend extra hours with her on the flight there and back.

Sean grinned. 'What can I say? When it comes to the ladies, I'm a genius.'

'Speaking of which, what's happening in your own love life? I've never known you to be single for long.'

'I told you. I've turned over a new leaf. For now, I'm concentrating on my studies and my career. No time for distractions.'

Darcy's eyebrows shot up. 'Since when did Casanova Howard not have time for a little R and R?'

To Darcy's surprise, Sean's expression turned serious. 'I've let you down before, bro. I won't do it again.' He paused, as if searching for the right words. 'I'm not like Dad, you know.'

Darcy could hardly believe his ears. He'd always assumed that Sean idolised their father because he'd tried to emulate him in so many ways: the transient lifestyle, moving from place to place, trying to find the next adventure, unwilling to accept responsibility. Yet here he was, admitting their dad wasn't the paragon of virtue he'd made him out to be.

'We've never spoken about this,' Darcy said, filled with pride at the man he'd raised Sean to be.

'Yeah, well, it isn't often we get heavy, is it? Besides, I haven't been around much over the years. And in case I haven't said this, thanks for looking after me, bro. I was a ratbag kid yet you never complained. Don't know how you put up with me.'

Darcy smiled, trying to lighten the moment before he turned into a total sap and tears sprung to his eyes. 'Well, somebody had to do it.' He slapped Sean on the back. 'Thanks for the advice. I'll give the airline a call right now.'

'Good luck.'

Darcy didn't need luck. Everything would fall into place and Fleur would make him the happiest man alive.

Fleur's last week at Innovative Imports flew by and before she knew it she'd packed up her belongings, said goodbye to the staff and prepared herself for the surprise dinner that Darcy had planned. She'd dressed to impress, wearing a low-cut fitted top, matching skirt and sequinned sandals; knowing Darcy's taste in restaurants, she didn't want to appear underdressed. Memories of their first dinner together at the Potter Lounge still left her feeling uncomfortable—she just wasn't cut out for that sort of lifestyle. Give her the local Italian pizzeria, with its noisy patrons, red and white checked tablecloths and home-cooked pasta any day.

Her doorbell rang as she snapped an earring into place and finished off with a liberal spray of her favourite perfume. Predictably, Darcy had arrived exactly at eight.

'Hi there...' Her greeting trailed off as she opened the door, stunned to find him wearing jeans and a polo shirt.

He wolf-whistled, long and low. 'You look great.'

'But obviously overdressed. See what happens when you don't tell me where we're going? Just give me a minute to change.'

'Uh, slight change of plan. Sorry.'

He didn't look sorry at all and her blood pressure rose a notch or two. 'What's that supposed to mean?'

'Dinner tonight has changed to breakfast tomorrow morning. At the airport. Is that OK?' He grinned, the smug look on his face not placating her at all. In fact, she had the distinct urge to wipe that self-satisfied smirk right off his face.

She folded her arms and gave him her best 'I'm not impressed' look. 'No, it's not OK. You could've called and let me know.' She didn't add 'before I went to all this trouble'.

Despite her intention to say goodbye to him tonight and get him out of her life once and for all, she'd wanted to leave a lasting impression and had managed to squeeze in a hairdresser's appointment and a manicure after work. Not to mention the hour she'd taken on her make-up.

'Where's the fun in that?'

Suddenly her patience snapped, the build-up of tension over the last few weeks reaching boiling point.

'I don't know what you're trying to prove but cancelling someone's plans by arriving on her doorstep isn't fun. It's downright rude. As for breakfast at the airport, I can't.'

Her tirade stunned him. His smile slipped and he reached out to her but she backed away. 'Breakfast is just a prelude to the main event. I've booked a mystery flight as a surprise. So, surprise!'

'You *what*?' Her voice rose to an un-ladylike shriek and she calmed it with effort. 'What made you think I'd fly any-where with you?'

A frown replaced his smile. 'You're the one who lives for the moment. I thought you'd love to do something spon-taneous like that.'

Suddenly, a sneaking suspicion insin-uated its way into her thoughts and quickly blossomed. 'Don't tell me. The motorbike, that weird yo-yo thingy and now this. Are you trying to tell me some-thing?'

He shrugged yet looked uncomfortable. 'It's no big deal. I just wanted to try a few new things, to look at life differently as you kept urging me to do.'

She shook her head, appalled that he'd made such an effort to impress her and she would slam the door on their rela-tionship anyway. 'You don't need to change for anybody, Darcy. You need to be your own person.'

'Then what was all that crap about learning to have fun?' He impaled her with a probing stare yet she didn't flinch.

'That was business.' She kept her tone deliberately light, wishing they didn't need to have this conversation.

'We moved to the personal stage a long time ago. Or was that just another of your *lessons*?' His bitterness cut her to the core, leaving her with an urge to bury herself in his arms for whatever comfort he could offer her.

'Don't do this, Darcy.'

'Do what? Fight for what I believe is right? Don't you get it? I'm in love with you, dammit! And you haven't got a clue.' He ran his hand through his hair, looking more flustered than she'd ever seen him.

It took a second for his words to penetrate her brain, but even then she could hardly believe them. He *loved* her? But he couldn't! This wasn't supposed to happen—they were all wrong for each other and there was no way she'd end up in a dead-end relationship for a fleeting taste of happiness now. What was the point, when they'd grow to hate each other or, worse still, grow old and complacent together like her parents?

She stared at him, trying to formulate the words to drive him away, her heart breaking.

He captured her face in his hands, moving too quickly for her to react. 'Go on, tell me you don't feel anything. Tell me I'm wrong about us.'

She tried to shake her head free but he held her firm. 'Tell me you don't love me.'

Though it was the hardest thing she'd ever had to do in her life, Fleur knew that this was her only chance even if it meant lying to him. Unable to meet the blazing intensity of his gaze, she looked away and whispered the two words guaranteed to drive him away.

'I don't.'

CHAPTER ELEVEN

THOUGH Springwood was the last place Fleur would have chosen to visit at a time like this, her mother seemed to have a sixth sense for trouble and had phoned her last night, just as Darcy walked out of her life. Unable to hide her emotions, she'd burst into tears as soon as her mum had said hello and the rest was history. Before she'd known what was happening, she'd agreed to head home for the weekend for some old-fashioned pampering and, strangely enough, as she turned into her parents' driveway she looked forward to it.

The claustrophobic dread that enveloped her whenever she returned home had vanished, leaving in its wake a sense of relief that here was one place on earth she could mend her broken heart in peace. Surprisingly, her folks didn't come flying out the door as they usually did, smothering her with their own brand of love. Instead, her mum answered the door when Fleur knocked.

'Come in, love. Your dad's in town.'

And just like that, she flew into her mother's welcoming arms, comforted by the familiar smells of rose essence mixed with baking, smells of her childhood which she'd never fully appreciated until now.

'Thanks for this, Mum. I really needed a break.' Fleur pulled away and dabbed at her eyes, tired of wiping away tears. That's all she'd been doing for the last twenty-four hours, blubbering like a two-year-old.

'You're welcome any time, dear. This is your home.' She bustled Fleur into the kitchen and set about making tea, her panacea for all ills.

Fleur took a seat at the kitchen table and looked around, taking in the old wooden dresser that had belonged to her great-grandmother, the chipped porcelain plates her mum collected and the odd assortment of mugs that seemed to grow with every passing year—and it suddenly hit her. This *was* home—her home—and she'd never really taken notice of it, shunning its familiarity in search of something bigger and better, always eager to escape.

'Mum, how did you put up with me?'

Her mother smiled and placed a cup of tea and a plate of her homemade scones in front of her. 'You're my daughter. I didn't have much choice, did I?'

'But I was such a pain! Probably still am,' she mumbled as she took a sip of tea.

Her mother sat down beside her and placed a comforting hand on her shoulder. 'You wanted to spread your wings from an early age, dear. Remember that time you leaped off the hay bale and broke your arm? You were four years old and I knew then that you were a free spirit who wouldn't be confined to this small town.' She smiled and looked away, as if lost in her own memories. 'You told me that day you were trying to fly away with the kookaburras and that one day you'd do it.' She cupped her cheek. 'You had such a determined look on your face that I knew you'd eventually follow through with your dream and leave us.'

Tears welled in Fleur's eyes and she blinked them away. 'There's more to it than that, Mum.'

'I know. You think your father and I are stuck here in this dead-end town, stuck in our boring ways.'

Fleur blushed, flooded with remorse. 'Is it that obvious?'

Her mother chuckled. 'I may be old but I'm not senile.'

'I've made such a mess of things.' Whatever it took, Fleur would make amends with her parents. Now, if only mending the rest of her life was as simple.

As if sensing the direction of her thoughts, her mother asked, 'How's that man of yours?'

'He's not mine.' Which was exactly what she'd wanted. So why did she feel so darn awful?

'Would you like him to be?'

Fleur had asked herself that same question a million times and still wasn't prepared to answer honestly. 'I don't know.'

'He seemed to be the perfect gentleman. Not to mention extremely good-looking.' The twinkle in her mother's eye surprised Fleur. 'And I bet he's a master in the sack!'

'Mum!' Fleur couldn't believe her mother had just said that and she stared at her in disbelief.

'I'm not as ancient as you think I am, dear. Do you love him?'

Fleur wanted to scream 'yes' to the world, but she'd been denying it for so long that she couldn't quite accept it yet. 'I suppose so.'

'Then what's the problem?'

'We're too different. He's older, more set in his ways. I like my freedom. We'd end up hating each other.'

Her mum shook her head. 'Not necessarily. Look at your father and me.'

'Huh?'

A wry grin crossed her mother's face. 'Despite what you think, I was young once too. And I know exactly where your wanderlust comes from. Me.'

'You're kidding.' As if her mum mentioning sex wasn't bad enough, she was now admitting that she'd harboured the same rebellious streak to escape as Fleur experienced!

'No, I'm not. As you know, your father and I met in high school. He wanted to settle down, I didn't. So I lived in Sydney for a year, working, living...' She drifted off for a second, obviously lost in her memories as Fleur struggled not to gape. 'I had the best time, dear, and dated several men, but none of them was your father. So I came back, feeling more grounded and ready to have a life. A real life. There's nothing wrong with a steady man, one who will support you through life's ups and downs and just be there for you. After all, an exciting life doesn't last forever but a good man will.'

Fleur stared at her mother as if truly seeing her for the first time. She'd honed in on the problem with unerring accuracy, leaving Fleur stunned by her revelations and how she could apply them to her own life.

'Darcy is a good man,' Fleur managed to say, her throat choked with emotion.

'Then hang on to him and don't let go.' Her mum leaned over and hugged her as both shed a few tears.

'Thanks, Mum. For everything.' Fleur pulled away slowly and wondered if her mother had any idea how their shared confidences of this afternoon had changed their relationship for the better.

'I'm always here for you, darling. Always have been, always will be.'

Feeling as if a weight had been lifted from her shoulders, Fleur finished her tea while a multitude of thoughts swirled through her head.

She just hoped that it wasn't too late for her and Darcy.

Standing up and stretching his back, Darcy stood at his office window and looked out at the glittering lights of Melbourne. He'd been working like a maniac the last week, throwing himself into the business with renewed enthusiasm. Thanks to Fleur and her creative ideas, his company flourished once again and he couldn't be happier.

Then why the empty feeling that wouldn't quit?

Even now, a week after she'd closed the door in his face while simultaneously slamming the door on their relationship, he couldn't concentrate on tasks for long, his mind constantly drifting to what might have been. What if she'd loved him? What if he'd been a different person? What if they'd met years earlier?

Pointless, really, as 'what ifs' ended nowhere. Especially the latter one—hell, if they'd met ten years earlier, she would've been commencing high school! Of all the women he had to fall for, it had to be someone unobtainable, someone so focused on living life to the max that she wasn't ready for anything else.

He should've known better. He should've accepted what she'd been throwing in his face from the start. They were too different and all the changes in the world wouldn't make him a more attractive package to a woman like her.

Despite his heartache, a small part of him was grateful to her. He had loosened up considerably and was reaping the rewards. He actually enjoyed coming to work these days, the interaction with his staff a rewarding experience rather than a trial. And as for his Harley, it was his pride and joy and he never tired of riding around, indulging his rebellious streak that had lain dormant all these years.

A tentative knock sounded at the door and he swung around, surprised there was anyone left in the office. He'd been burning the midnight oil all this week and thought that everyone had left hours ago.

'Come in.'

'Mr Darcy Howard?' A courier stepped into the room and handed him an envelope. 'Urgent delivery. Sign here, please.'

'Nice to know someone else is working late,' Darcy said, wondering what was so urgent that couldn't have waited until the morning.

'Yeah, right,' the courier muttered, tucking the clipboard under his arm and walking out.

Darcy slit open the heavy cream envelope, curiosity building as he withdrew a matching sheet of paper and opened it.

OLIVIA'S ART GALLERY
PROUDLY INVITES YOU TO A
PRIVATE SHOWING

COMMENCING AT 10PM
OCTOBER 27TH
DRESS: CASUAL
SUPPER PROVIDED

He stared at the printed invitation and wondered what was so important about this private showing scheduled for to-morrow night that it had been couriered over. He perused several art galleries in Melbourne on a regular basis but he'd never heard of this one, though the ad-dress indicated it wasn't far from his of-fice. To make matters more intriguing, the invite didn't state the name of the art-ist showing their work.

Tossing it into his briefcase, he knew he'd probably attend the showing tomor-row night, out of curiosity more than anything else. After all, how else would he spend his time on a Saturday night?

*   *   *

'Are you sure you know what you're doing?' Liv asked for the hundredth time, fiddling with Fleur's hair before stepping back and taking a critical look.

'What have I got to lose? It's now or never.' Fleur glanced around, pleased with the ambiance created by the dimmed downlights, the few candles she'd lit and the rich drapes that shaded the windows from prying eyes.

'Don't get your hopes up. He mightn't show.'

Fleur shrugged, trying to downplay her nerves. 'If he doesn't, I'll just have to ring him and get him over here, one way or the other. Or else I'll turn up on his doorstep.'

Liv smiled and gave her a thumbs-up sign of encouragement. 'Girl, you've got more guts than me. Hope it works out for you.'

'So do I, Liv. So do I.'

Liv hugged her. 'Don't get too swept away in the romance of it all and forget to lock up, will you?'

'Don't worry. Now go. He should be here soon.'

Liv blew her a kiss on her way out, leaving Fleur alone with her thoughts. And misgivings. She'd come up with this harebrained scheme on the way back from Springwood, knowing she needed a novel way to capture Darcy's attention. After all the trouble he'd gone to to impress her she needed to make an equally powerful statement, and what better way than this? He loved art galleries, though she fully intended to give him a showing tonight he'd never forget.

As if thoughts of the man had conjured him up, she heard the tinkling of the bell indicating the arrival of someone pushing open the front door. Taking a deep breath to calm her nerves, she peeked around the curtain that separated the gallery from the back room. Though she'd psyched herself up for this meeting, the sight of Darcy clad in black jeans and T-shirt sent her imagination into overdrive and she could barely restrain herself from running into his arms. He looked amazing, better than she remembered and it had only been a week.

'Hello? Anyone here?' He looked around the gallery and she could see the frown on his brow.

Adjusting her dress one last time, she stepped from behind the curtain, prepared to play the role of a lifetime to try and win back the man of her dreams.

CHAPTER TWELVE

'GLAD you could come.' Fleur walked towards Darcy, head held high. She needed to project some confidence before she bolted back behind the curtain in embarrassment.

'What are you doing here?' He stared at her as if he'd seen a ghost.

She shrugged, as if she did this every day of the week. 'I know how much you like art galleries and I thought you might be interested in a particular piece this one has on offer.'

His frown deepened, sending her meagre supply of self-confidence spiralling downwards. 'Have you lost your mind?'

'No, actually I've come to my senses. Please, won't you follow me?' She strolled to the door on jelly-like legs and locked it, knowing they couldn't be disturbed for what she had in mind.

'I'm not in the mood for games, Fleur. Haven't you played enough of them?'

In response, she took hold of his hand, prepared to drag him into the back room if necessary. However, he came willingly and her heart thudded in her chest as the magnitude of what she was about to do hit home.

What if he wanted out, even after tonight? She couldn't bear being apart from him for one more day—the last week had been agonising. She'd never thought she could miss another person that much, never thought she could love a man as much as she loved Darcy. And she had to prove it to him, one way or another.

'What the hell is going on here?' He balked at the doorway as she pulled the curtain aside, stepped into the back room and out of her dress, trying to act as if she stripped for a man every day of the week.

'It's a private showing, remember?'

His eyes gleamed in the candlelight, their expression unreadable. 'This isn't a good idea, Fleur.'

'Oh, no?' Mustering the last of her courage, she stood on tiptoe and pressed her body against his, all too aware of the minimal barrier of clothes between them.

He didn't move a muscle as she laid her hands on his chest, revelling in the hard contours of his body as she slid them upwards.

'I thought you didn't want this. Us.' He'd stilled and she heard his sharp intake of breath.

'I was wrong.' She wrapped her hands around his neck and pulled his head down, breathless with anticipation. 'And what better way to make it up to you?'

He opened his mouth as if to answer her but she didn't let him speak, covering his lips with hers, putting her heart and soul into the kiss. She clutched at his shoulders and arched towards him, needing to prove how much she wanted him, now and forever.

Her grip tightened as she felt him pull away. 'Darcy, please—'

'No, this can't happen.' He unlinked her hands from behind his head and stepped away. 'And put something on.'

Blinking back tears, she zipped up her dress and wondered where to go from here. She'd envisaged them making passionate love followed by an honest talk about their future together. However, she hadn't counted on the man being made of stone—after all, he'd hardly resisted her in the past and if she couldn't convince him of her love by showing him with her body, what chance did she have by using her mind?

'Fancy some supper?' She'd done this her whole life, trying to lighten up tense situations with pathetic attempts at humour. 'I'm serving humble pie.'

He didn't laugh. 'What's all this about, Fleur?'

She sank onto a nearby chair, suddenly struck by a bone-deep weariness. Who had she been trying to kid? She couldn't pull this off—and the man she loved would walk straight out the door and out of her life any second now.

'I thought we should talk.'

'Don't you think you've said enough?'

She clasped her hands and rested them in her lap—anything to stop their constant fiddling. Another bad habit she had when she was nervous. 'I haven't been completely honest with you.'

He didn't reply and she looked up, seeing impatience written all over his face.

Trying not to babble, she continued, 'The last time I saw you, you said you loved me. And I denied having any feelings for you. Well, that wasn't entirely true.' She cleared her throat, wishing her voice didn't sound so squeaky. 'I do. Have feelings for you. In fact, I've fallen in love with you.'

An awkward silence stretched between them and she wished he would say something, anything, to relieve her growing apprehension. Instead, he just stood there, staring at her and not moving a muscle.

'So, what do you want me to do about it?' She jumped when he finally spoke, his words shredding the last of her confidence.

'I— I thought you might like to pick up where we left off and—'

'Forget it,' he cut in. 'I've had enough of trying to prove myself to you. Nothing I did was good enough. What makes you think anything would be different now? I'm still the same man and, from what I can see, you haven't changed a bit.' His lip curled in what only could be described as derision and she flinched.

'What's that supposed to mean?'

'All this.' He gestured around the room. 'You're still playing games or trying to live in a fantasy world; I just haven't figured out which yet. If you really wanted to talk, why didn't you come by the house?' He shook his head, looking thoroughly disgusted. 'But that would've been too *boring* for you, wouldn't it? You need excitement in your life, a challenge, anything to give you a thrill. Well, sorry, lady, I'm just not interested any more.'

'You don't understand. I've changed.' Her voice came out a whisper as a lone tear trickled down her cheek.

'Save it for someone who cares.' He turned on his heel and walked out, leaving her in a flood of tears and lamenting the loss of what might have been.

Liv had been the perfect friend, consoling Fleur with constant distractions. However, now that a month had passed since the debacle with Darcy at the art gallery, Fleur knew she had to get on with her life and stop being such a wet blanket. Starting with their lunch date today.

'Hey, gorgeous. Here's that cappuccino you ordered.' Billy winked at her as he placed the foaming coffee in front of her and she actually managed a smile.

'Thanks, Billy.'

'Haven't seen you around much. Bet you ditched me for another fella.'

'No chance. Who else makes coffee like this?' She took a sip, savouring the rich flavour of the beans and needing the caffeine hit.

'That's what they all say.' He rolled his eyes. 'I'd better get back to work. Nice to have you back, kiddo.'

As Billy strolled to the counter, she wondered if she'd been that much of a recluse. Sure, the money she'd earned from Darcy's job had taken the pressure off, leaving her free for another month or so if she wished, but had it really been that long since she'd been in here?

'Hello, stranger. Fancy seeing you here.' Liv plopped into the seat opposite, answering Fleur's question without knowing it.

'It hasn't been that long?'

'Girl, even the grizzlies hibernate for shorter periods than you!'

'I wasn't hibernating. I was mending a broken heart. Totally different circumstances.' Fleur managed a chuckle, which proved how far she'd come.

'How's all that coming along?' Liv's smile waned as she tipped two sugars into her coffee and stirred it.

'Better. Thanks to you.'

'Hey, I didn't do that much.'

'You did enough. Thanks, Liv.'

Liv blushed. 'Yeah, well, you helped me too.'

'How?'

'I've given up on romance. It's nothing like the books say it is. It sucks!'

Fleur grinned. 'Just because things didn't work out between Darcy and me doesn't mean that romance is all that bad.'

'But you two were so great together...' Liv trailed off, looking decidedly uncomfortable. 'Anyway, let's not talk about that. What are your plans now? Any jobs in the pipeline?'

Fleur nodded. 'I did get some information in the mail the other day. Some new company starting up would like me in on the ground level to make sure they get the staffing right.'

'Sounds promising. You going to take it?'

'Probably.' Fleur stared at the dregs in her coffee cup, thinking that her life resembled them. Nothing held any appeal any more, especially not work. It reminded her of her last job, which had her back on the same old emotional merry-go-round as memories of Darcy flooded back.

'I think you should do it. Consider it part of Liv's formula for ridding the system of unwanted baggage.'

And suddenly, Fleur knew Liv was right. She had to stop moping around and get her life back on track; she'd wasted enough time wallowing in self-pity.

'You're right. I'll follow up that contact first thing in the morning.' Even saying the words out loud seemed to inject a spark of enthusiasm into her. Life had to go on, with or without the likes of Darcy Howard.

'That's more like it. Now, what's for lunch?'

As Liv perused the menu, Fleur breathed a sigh of relief. She was back and it was time to start acting like it.

Fleur donned the black designer suit she'd purchased as part of Liv's 'retail therapy programme', took extra care with her hair and make-up and picked up her new handbag. She could hardly recognise her reflection in the mirror—she'd spent the last month bumming around the apartment in tracksuit trousers and sloppy T-shirts, looking and feeling like a reject. About time she stepped back into the real world, and what better way to do it than looking like a million dollars?

She drove into the city, trying to recall the few details she'd gleaned about this new company. Apart from the name, How Now, which didn't tell her much, she knew they planned on franchising their business. The request for her input had come in writing and there had been no phone number, which had struck her as odd. However, their letterhead looked official enough and she'd faxed them her response, stating her intention to meet with them at their downtown office at ten a.m. today.

She arrived with five minutes to spare and took the lift to the fifteenth floor, impressed by the new building and large floor space. Money couldn't be a problem for this company, for she knew the lease rates in this part of town were exorbitant. Pushing through heavy glass doors, she noticed the office hadn't been fitted out yet, adding to the illusion of space. Starting at the ground level would be a challenge and she couldn't wait to meet the owner of this venture and get down to business.

'Hello?' she called out, her voice echoing through the room.

'Glad you could make it.' A tall male stepped out from one of the smaller offices and she gaped.

'Sean? What are you doing here?' Her mind spun with the implications of his presence at this office and she hoped that he was the only Howard brother in attendance.

'Good to see you too.' He chuckled and moved towards her, holding out his hand. 'Welcome to my new venture. What do you think so far?'

Play it cool, girl. There had been no mention of Darcy and there was no way she'd be foolish enough to ask if he was involved in this project.

'Nice office. Very upmarket.'

'A bit like you these days. Great suit.' His admiring glance slid over her, making her feel proud rather than uncomfortable. Both Howard brothers had class, she'd give them that much.

'Thanks. So, what's all this about?'

'Come into my office and we can discuss it.'

She followed him into a small office with the bare essentials: a desk, two chairs and a fax machine.

'As you can see, I'm in the middle of fitting out this place. But this will do for now.' He sat in the chair opposite and folded his arms, a strange, smug look on his face. 'How have you been?'

'Not bad.' Hah! Understatement of the year—she'd been downright awful, not that she'd let him know. Wouldn't Darcy just love that, to find out she'd been pining away for him?

'Tell me about the business.' She needed to get this meeting on track before Sean asked any more inquisitive personal questions, questions she had no intention of answering.

'Still the same old Fleur, huh? Ready to grab the world with both hands and give it a mighty shake-up.'

'Nothing wrong with ambition. Look at you.'

Sean grinned. 'Yeah, the prodigal son returns and becomes CEO. Who would've guessed?'

Fleur smiled politely, tiring of the small talk. She wanted to get down to business. 'About the company?'

'Oh, that.' He waved her prompt away as if it meant little. 'I'll leave you to discuss the details with my project manager. And here he comes now.'

Fleur swivelled in her chair, stood up and held out her hand, eager to meet the man who could set the wheels in motion.

'Sean, what the hell is going on here?'

Fleur's heart sank and her hand dropped uselessly to her side as she stared at the man she'd been trying so hard to forget.

CHAPTER THIRTEEN

'WELL? I asked you a question.' Darcy glowered at Sean, studiously avoiding looking at Fleur.

'I'm doing you a favour.' Sean smirked, looking as though he was thoroughly enjoying himself. 'You could be more gracious about it.'

'This isn't funny.'

'Who says?' Sean stood up and made for the door. 'Now, if you'll excuse me, I think you two have important business to discuss.'

'We have nothing to discuss.' Darcy finally risked a glance at Fleur, knowing he shouldn't have. She'd paled, her dark eyes standing out like beacons in her face, and he curbed his first reaction to rush over, envelop her in his arms and comfort her. For that was exactly what she looked as though she needed—someone to pick her up, cradle her in their arms and whisper platitudes that everything was going to be all right.

'Is this some kind of joke?' Fleur stared at both of them, contempt mixed with loathing blazing from her eyes.

Darcy tried to stare her down, knowing he deserved some of that loathing but it hurt none the less. And it shouldn't, dammit! It had been over a month since he'd laid eyes on her and he'd steeled himself to forget her. It hadn't been easy but he'd been getting there. Until now. Seeing her again had slammed into his gut like a punch, leaving him floundering, strangely breathless and feeling slightly nauseous.

Sean shook his head. 'Sorry, Fleur. No joke, but this was the only way I could think of to get you two together.'

'But why?'

And just like that, Darcy knew she'd been feeling as bad as he had. Her anguished cry reverberated off the walls, penetrating the barriers he'd erected against her, leaving him shaken.

'Because you love each other and you owe it to yourselves to sort this mess out.' Sean spoke quietly, confidently, as if stating the obvious. 'And besides, I'm sick of living with *him* in this state. He's completely insane.'

'You're way out of line,' Darcy said, watching the last of the colour leech from Fleur's face. 'Now get out.'

'Anything you say, bro.' Sean pushed past him in the doorway. 'And don't screw up this time!'

Darcy waited till Sean had stepped into the lift before turning his attention to Fleur. She'd sunk back into her seat, looking faint.

'I'm sorry about all this. I had no idea,' he said, her fragility scaring him.

What had happened to the tough, rambunctious girl who wouldn't let anything or anyone stand in her way? The Fleur he'd known would've laughed this episode off, putting it down to Sean's bizarre sense of humour.

She looked up, fixing him with a sad gaze that invoked every protective mechanism he possessed. 'It's not your fault.'

And suddenly, he knew that wasn't true. This whole disastrous mess *was* his fault. He'd been too stubborn, too proud, too stuck in his ways to forgive and forget. Even when she'd declared she loved him, he'd pushed her away, his ego still smarting from her earlier rejection. He'd used every excuse in the book over the last month to push her memory aside: she was too fickle, too young, too much like his own parents, who'd lived by the seat of their pants with little time or love left over for him.

And he'd been afraid. In fact, he'd been downright terrified that if he took a chance on loving her, she'd hurt him as much as they had, leaving him alone in the end.

Ironic, really, as that was exactly how he'd ended up anyway. Alone. And hurting like hell.

'Maybe Sean's right. We do need to talk.' He held his breath, wondering if the sudden flicker of hope in her eyes had been a figment of his imagination.

'Is there really anything left to say?'

He crossed the room and perched on the edge of the desk, close enough for her signature scent to reach out and envelop him, dragging him under her spell all over again, resurrecting a host of memories he'd carefully suppressed.

'It may not be too late for us.' There, he'd said it and she merely stared at him, not responding in the slightest. 'I've been stupid, Fleur. That night at the art gallery, I acted like a pompous old fool and I'm sorry. Really sorry.' He shook his head, feeling like the world's biggest moron. 'You said you loved me and I threw that back in your face. When in fact, I should've—'

'What?'

'Done this.' He slid down onto his knees, pulled her into his arms and kissed her, groaning in relief as his mouth settled over hers. He'd ached for this, longed for it, needing to feel the sweetness of her mouth flowering under his.

Fleur should've struggled, should've pushed him away. However, the minute he touched her, she knew. This was where she belonged, now and forever.

She responded by parting her lips, letting his tongue slide in, stroking hers, teasing her to match his passion as her arms slid around his torso, hanging on with every intention of never letting go. His hands were everywhere, skimming her breasts, tangling in her hair, exploring every inch of her as the latent desire between them sparked in an instant, exploding into a roaring inferno that threatened to burn out of control and consume them both.

Hanging on to the last of her self-control by a thread, she broke the kiss and backed away from his embrace. 'We're not doing much talking.'

'You're one hell of a distraction.' He dropped a kiss on the end of her nose and released her, remaining on his knees in front of her. 'But you're right. We should talk.'

She took a steadying breath, not quite believing they were having this conversation. 'My feelings haven't changed.'

'Nor have mine.' He stared into her eyes and her heart flip-flopped at the love she glimpsed there.

'So, where do we go from here?'

'How about we try a relationship? A real, honest-to-goodness relationship, with no lessons to be learned, no points to prove? And if you really need it, no strings attached?'

Her heart sank. 'Why no strings attached?'

He took hold of her hands. 'I know we're very different. And I recognise your need for freedom even if I don't necessarily agree with it. I'd rather share part of your life than none at all, so if you want out at any stage, tell me and I'll deal with it.'

'You'd do that for me?' She couldn't believe her ears. Could he love her so much that he would willingly sacrifice his own happiness for her?

'I love you.' He shrugged, as if it was the simplest thing in the world. 'Sure, my life has been quiet and dull in comparison to yours but I wanted it that way. I lost my parents at an early age thanks to their carefree attitude to life and I responded by shutting down my own emotions. Why live life to the fullest when it only ends in pain? Your attitude reminded me of them and, though I wanted you more than anything, I wasn't willing to put my heart on the line and risk being hurt again, especially as you'd already knocked me back once.' He squeezed her hands. 'So, in answer to your question, yes, I'd do that for you. I won't be responsible for stifling you or trying to change you. I love you just the way you are.'

She didn't bother blinking back the tears, letting them trickle down her cheeks. 'You're incredible. I was so busy comparing you to *my* parents, I didn't stop to realise that being a steady, responsible person isn't such a bad thing after all. In fact, I want that life. I want *you*. All of you.'

'Even though I'm old, stodgy, dull and boring?' He grinned and wiped away her tears.

'Forget I ever said that. You're the most wonderful man I've ever met and I'll love you forever.' She clasped his face in her hands and placed a gentle kiss on his lips. 'And you can forget about that no-strings-attached business. You're stuck with me now.'

'Well, in that case, while I'm down here...' He squared his shoulders and grabbed her hands, holding on tightly as if he would never let go. 'Fleur, will you marry me?'

She stared at him in disbelief, overcome with an emotion she never thought she'd experience—love had sneaked up on her and, despite her best intentions to hold it at arm's length, she'd succumbed. 'Yes!'

'In that case, come here and give your *old* fiancé a big kiss.' He pulled her into his arms, the only place in the world she wanted to be.

EPILOGUE

'SO MUCH for a conventional wedding!' Liv clambered out of the sidecar and tried to smooth her satin dress.

'But you hate convention,' Fleur said, tugging at her veil and making sure it wouldn't fly away in the breeze. 'In fact, wasn't it your idea to hire the Harleys to get us here in the first place?'

'Maybe,' Liv blushed, 'but that was before I knew so many men would be here, and I must look a mess. Look around, girlfriend. It's wall-to-wall hunks out here. Darcy sure has some scrumptious friends.'

'You're supposed to be helping me, not drooling over the guys. Besides, there's plenty of time for that later at the reception. Right now, I need you.'

Liv rolled her eyes after managing to drag her stare away from a group of men in tuxedos. 'It's all about you. How about you concentrate on getting up that aisle and I concentrate on finding a fella to do the same with?'

'Sean will be here soon.'

'So?' Liv's blush deepened and Fleur grinned. Ever since the two had met, Liv had pretended that she didn't give a damn about Darcy's brother, a sure sign that she had the hots for him, big-time.

'Just thought you'd like to know. After all, it's normal for the maid of honour and the best man to co-ordinate itineraries, make sure everything goes smoothly, get drunk and make out at the reception...'

'Shh! Someone might hear you.' Liv glanced around in a panic and Fleur knew, without a doubt, that Sean was in trouble. Her friend never acted this flustered unless she really liked a guy.

'And that would be a bad thing because?'

'Come on, let's get you married off.' Liv tucked a stray curl behind Fleur's tiara and fiddled with her crystal earrings. 'Then you can make Darcy's life a misery instead of mine.'

'You can't get rid of me that easily.' Fleur smiled and planted a quick peck on her friend's cheek. 'Thanks for all your help, Liv. I couldn't have done it without you.'

'Yeah, yeah, the story of my life. Always the bridesmaid, never a bride.' Liv hugged Fleur. 'But you're welcome. Now let's go. Darcy will be waiting.'

Taking a deep breath, Fleur crossed the lawn to where her father waited patiently.

'Ready, petal?'

'Ready as I'll ever be, Dad.'

'Off we go, then.' He tucked her hand into the crook of his elbow and waited for the first strains of the music.

Though they had broken with tradition for most of their wedding, Fleur had insisted that her father walk her up the aisle or, in this case, the red carpet that lay over the grass of her parents' property. It was a small gesture but one she'd wanted to make as a demonstration of her love for the man she'd misjudged all these years.

Once the string quartet started up, Liv winked at Fleur and sauntered up the aisle, a vision in royal-blue satin.

'It's our turn.' Her dad squeezed her hand as they followed behind and Fleur looked ahead, eager to catch the first glimpse of her groom.

As they rounded the old oak tree she had used to swing on as a child, she saw him, standing as straight as a soldier in front of the minister on the bank of the creek. The gasps of awe and muttered twitterings from the guests barely registered as she strolled towards him, her gaze fixed on the man about to become her husband.

'She's all yours.' Her dad placed her hand in Darcy's and she smiled, basking in the admiration of his stare.

'Are you having fun yet?' Darcy whispered in her ear as he bent to place a kiss on her cheek.

She turned her head at the last minute, bringing her lips flush with his before whispering against the side of his mouth, 'Sweetheart, for us, the fun's only just beginning.'

MILLS & BOON® PUBLISH EIGHT LARGE PRINT TITLES A MONTH. THESE ARE THE EIGHT TITLES FOR OCTOBER 2005

———— ❦ ————

MARRIED BY ARRANGEMENT
Lynne Graham

PREGNANCY OF REVENGE
Jacqueline Baird

IN THE MILLIONAIRE'S POSSESSION
Sara Craven

THE ONE-NIGHT WIFE
Sandra Marton

THE ITALIAN'S RIGHTFUL BRIDE
Lucy Gordon

HUSBAND BY REQUEST
Rebecca Winters

CONTRACT TO MARRY
Nicola Marsh

THE MIRRABROOK MARRIAGE
Barbara Hannay

MILLS & BOON®

Live the emotion

0905 Rom LP

MILLS & BOON® PUBLISH EIGHT LARGE PRINT TITLES A MONTH. THESE ARE THE EIGHT TITLES FOR NOVEMBER 2005

BOUGHT: ONE BRIDE
Miranda Lee

HIS WEDDING RING OF REVENGE
Julia James

BLACKMAILED INTO MARRIAGE
Lucy Monroe

THE GREEK'S FORBIDDEN BRIDE
Cathy Williams

PREGNANT: FATHER NEEDED
Barbara McMahon

A NANNY FOR KEEPS
Liz Fielding

THE BRIDAL CHASE
Darcy Maguire

MARRIAGE LOST AND FOUND
Trish Wylie

MILLS & BOON®

Live the emotion